Here's what critics are saying about Leslie Langtry's books:

"I laughed so hard I cried on multiple occasions while reading MARSHMALLOW S'MORE MURDER! Girl Scouts, the CIA, and the Yakuza... what could possibly go wrong?"
—Fresh Fiction

"Darkly funny and wildly over the top, this mystery answers the burning question, 'Do assassin skills and Girl Scout merit badges mix…' one truly original and wacky novel!"
—RT BOOK REVIEWS

"Those who like dark humor will enjoy a look into the deadliest female assassin and PTA mom's life."
—Parkersburg News

"Mixing a deadly sense of humor and plenty of sexy sizzle, Leslie Langtry creates a brilliantly original, laughter-rich mix of contemporary romance and suspense in *'Scuse Me While I Kill This Guy.*"
—Chicago Tribune

"The beleaguered soccer mom assassin concept is a winner, and Langtry gets the fun started from page one with a myriad of clever details."
—Publisher's Weekly

D1522023

BOOKS BY LESLIE LANGTRY

Merry Wrath Mysteries:
Merit Badge Murder
Mint Cookie Murder
Scout Camp Murder
(short story in the Killer Beach Reads collection)
Marshmallow S'More Murder
Movie Night Murder
Mud Run Murder
Fishing Badge Murder
(short story in the Pushing Up Daisies collection)
Motto for Murder

Greatest Hits Mysteries:
'Scuse Me While I Kill This Guy
Guns Will Keep Us Together
Stand By Your Hitman
I Shot You Babe
Paradise By The Rifle Sights
Snuff the Magic Dragon
My Heroes Have Always Been Hitmen
Have Yourself a Deadly Little Christmas (a holiday short story)

Aloha Lagoon Mysteries:
Ukulele Murder
Ukulele Deadly

Other Works:
Sex, Lies, & Family Vacations

MOTTO FOR MURDER

a Merry Wrath Mystery

Leslie Langtry

MOTTO FOR MURDER

CHAPTER ONE

────────

"Is that a dead body?" I asked Philby as I looked out the garage window.

Philby didn't answer because 1) she's rude like that, and 2) she's a cat. Still, she could flick her tail or something to show she agreed with me.

Next door, in the darkness, I saw my neighbors carrying what looked a lot like a body from their detached garage to their back door. It was quite a coincidence, really. I was taking the trash out and found my cat throwing herself at the small window as if a giant mouse made of albacore tuna was dancing just out of reach on the other side.

Philby gave me a long look, implying that I was an idiot for stating the obvious. But then, she looked like Hitler, so she wasn't allowed to judge me. The lights came on inside the neighbors' house, but I only saw two people silhouetted on the shade.

"Well," I said to my cat, "obviously they aren't going to lift the body and use it like a puppet just so we can see it."

Philby looked at me as if to say that normal people would do just that. Kind of like she does when she catches and kills a mouse. Cats think they know everything.

I pulled out my cell and called my fiancé, Detective Rex Ferguson, who lived across the street.

"Merry?" he asked. He sounded sleepy. I could've walked across the street and woken him up in person, but that seemed a little inconvenient to me.

"I think the neighbors killed a guy and carried him into their house!" I kept my voice quiet and my eyes on the window.

"What time is it?" Rex replied as though he heard this kind of thing all the time from me.

"I don't know." I squinted at the phone. "One o'clock. In the morning."

I'm not sure why I added that last bit, because obviously it was in the early morning, and Rex was a detective capable of determining that on his own.

"You're dreaming," he mumbled. "Go back to bed."

"Why would I be dreaming in my garage? Besides, I don't have neighbors on the other side of my house where the bedroom is. I'm wide awake and looking at them right now."

I pictured him rubbing his eyes. "Maybe whoever they were carrying was sick. Or inebriated. Do you have anything else to go on?"

"I think I know a dead body when I see one," I replied.

I regretted those words as soon as I said them. Why? Because I'd been found with a number of dead bodies over the last two years—bodies that had no connection to me. And no, I didn't kill them.

"Is this a formal complaint?" Rex asked.

I could tell he was debating whether it was worth getting out of bed to investigate.

"Yes!" I insisted. "They're probably cutting the dead guy up in the bathtub right now. You can catch them red-handed!"

"You do realize that if I go over there, the Fontanas are going to know it was you who tipped them off."

"You know their name?" How did he know them? I'd lived here longer than he had, and I didn't know them.

"Mark and Pam," he said. "They borrowed an egg from me a month ago. Nice people."

My spy-dy senses went haywire. "Don't you think that's suspicious? Two people borrowing one egg?"

"No, I don't." This conversation was finished as far as he was concerned. "I'll send a squad car over."

"What? No! You're the detective! *You* should go."

"I'm not going. For one thing, it isn't an investigation. An officer will suffice. And secondly, they're my neighbors. I don't want to freak them out with a full-on investigation of a murder when the only witness is…unreliable."

"Unreliable? I was a spy for the CIA for eight years! I'd say that makes me pretty reliable."

I could almost hear him shaking his head. "And you haven't slept in days. That means you could be hallucinating."

He's right. I haven't slept well for weeks. For some reason, insomnia had set in a month earlier, right before Valentine's Day. I'd been so tired I'd almost left the house in a red dress and combat boots.

"I don't think I'm hallucinating," I muttered. Just to be sure, I pinched Philby, who hissed and ran away. Nope, not asleep.

"Go to bed, Merry," Rex said firmly. "I'll send someone over."

He hung up before I could say anything else.

Now, a normal person might have gone to bed like their significant other said. But my adrenaline was spiking, so I ran to the living room, turned out the lights, and hid behind a curtain, waiting for the squad car to arrive.

There were several theories about my insomnia. Kelly, my best friend and co-leader of our Girl Scout troop, thought I was having pre-wedding jitters. I told her that technically, it couldn't be pre-wedding jitters since we hadn't even picked a date yet.

As for everyone else, Rex thought I was just plain crazy, and the four Kaitlyns in my Girl Scout troop announced that I was obviously suffering under the delusion that I was a vegetarian, pink bald eagle with glittery wings.

They were probably all right. When I did sleep, I imagined I was a pink eagle with glittery wings. I wondered how they knew.

Kelly was right. I was avoiding plans for the wedding. Why? Because I wasn't sure I was ready for this huge step. I'd only been engaged for five months. And during that time, a close friend had betrayed me and my former handler had vanished into thin air.

Thinking about Riley made my stomach drop into my knees. I'd made the right choice by choosing Rex. Besides, Riley hadn't proposed. Not that I'd wanted him to. Rex was my fiancé and I loved him. And I could count on him. And I trusted him.

The same couldn't be said for Riley. Not after the stunt he'd pulled.

Kelly said that once I picked a date, I'd feel better. I knew she was right. All this wedding stuff was too overwhelming. My best friend told me this was what I subconsciously wanted or I wouldn't have bought a minivan.

By the way, I bought a minivan. My little sedan wasn't able to transport my troop, so I bought something bigger. And no, this wasn't because Rex and I were going to start having kids. It was for the troop. Besides, if I ever bought something big, like a moose head or dresser, I'd have a vehicle big enough to take it home.

My parents thought I was freaking out over nothing. There'd been endless text messages from my mother in DC, who was more than thrilled to help me sort through all this wedding stuff. Since I was the only child of Senator Michael Czrygy and my glamorous mother, Judith Wrath Czrygy, they were excited to help. Maybe I should turn it over to her? Or let Kelly handle things.

The squad car turned the corner in front of my house and slowly crept forward to my neighbors', the Fontanas', house.

"No!" I whispered to no one. Philby and her kitten, Martini, were apparently done with me. "Not Kevin!"

The officer in question stepped out of the car with all the speed of a lobotomized sloth in a coma. He wiped his Cheetos-stained hands on his shirt and walked up to the door of the house.

Kevin Dooley and I had a history. And by history, I mean we'd gone to the same elementary school, where he'd been a well-known paste eater. The man never spoke. I'd always assumed he was hired because the police department had to hire a paste eater for diversity purposes.

But the police department in a small town like Who's There, Iowa had to take what they could get. And Kevin's dad had once been the head of security at the local hospital. He pulled some strings and voila! A paste-eating cop. Not that he ate paste anymore. He mostly was found with cheese puffs or powdered donuts. He was always eating.

I watched as he rang the doorbell. A few seconds later, a man in a bathrobe answered. The two men exchanged too few words to constitute an actual investigation. Then something surprising happened. Mr. Fontana invited Kevin inside.

I ran back out to the garage and watched as three silhouettes talked to each other. Two people walked away, and five minutes later, they were back—just enough time for me to scrounge up some Pizza Rolls. Five minutes after that, I watched Officer Dooley leave, get into his car, and drive away.

Why would Rex send Kevin? I guess he didn't believe me. This did nothing to help my insomnia, and I spent the rest of the night pacing the living room, trying to think of what to do. Part of me wanted to do some hardcore window peeping. But if the Fontanas spotted me and called the cops, I'd be busted.

Instead, I had a glass of wine, a hot bath, and four sleeping pills. By some small miracle, with the image of a vegetarian bald eagle carrying a body away, I drifted off to sleep.

CHAPTER TWO

My name is Merry Wrath. Actually, it's Fionnaghuala Merrygold Czrygy. Two years earlier I'd been "accidentally" outed as a field operative by the vice president of the United States—as a not too subtle act of revenge against my dad, who's a prominent senator from Iowa.

After receiving an amazingly huge settlement from the government, I'd changed my name and appearance and quietly come back to my hometown to sort myself out. Most people would take time to reflect on what they wanted to do next. Others would jump right into a new job.

I'd started a Girl Scout troop.

Unfortunately, over the past two years, dead bodies had inconveniently popped up around me. I hadn't murdered any of them but had discovered a knack for investigating that impressed my troop of 4th graders and frustrated my fiancé.

"I don't suppose you know how to plan a wedding, do you?" I asked my cats first thing in the morning. Being that we were in the kitchen and I was in the middle of giving them breakfast—they refused to answer.

Philby responded by belching, and Martini farted. I wasn't sure how to take that advice.

"You have to set a date first." A man's voice made me jump and land in a defensive stance.

Rex stepped into the kitchen from the living room. I relaxed because, in all fairness, he had a key to my house.

"What are you doing here?" I ran my fingers through my hair in a vain attempt to look presentable.

The cats walked over to Rex and demanded to be petted. And because they'd trained him well, he did. A few seconds later, both returned to their tuna after giving me an angry look that implied they wanted me to get a move on too. Maybe they were angling to be bridesmaids.

"You don't have to take his side," I protested.

Rex pulled me into a very toe-tingling kiss. "There aren't any sides, Merry. The date can be tomorrow or a year from now. I'd just like to know."

My fiancé was an unreasonably attractive man with a completely reasonable way of dealing with adult things. A few inches taller than my 5'9", he had short black hair, beautiful eyes, and a body most women would melt over. How did I get so lucky? I wasn't much to look at with my short, curly dirty-blonde hair and an affinity for junk food and sweat suits.

"I think we should tell your parents first," I said.

I'd only recently learned that his parents actually existed and lived nearby in the big city of Des Moines. He'd never mentioned family before, so I'd assumed he sprang forth, fully formed, from Zeus's head.

My suggestion had the desired effect. "We will." Rex released me and sighed. "It just has to be the right time."

"I'm outing myself for this wedding."

Okay, by "outing" I meant my parents were coming for the wedding and people would find out I was really Finn Czrygy. Not Merry Wrath—a disguise I'd invented so no one would bother me after the media madness that happened when I was *really* outed.

I was still going to use Merry Wrath because it sounded way cooler than an unpronounceable name like Fionnaghuala (which is spelled weird, since it's pronounced "finella") Czrygy. People would know who I really was when they saw my parents' names on the wedding program. I'd tried to argue that we didn't need programs but was shot down by Kelly, who insisted we did. Since she's smarter than me in these kinds of things, I'd acquiesced.

"I know. And I never asked you to do that," Rex continued.

Putting my hands on my hips in an attempt to appear intimidating, I said, "I've never met your parents. In fact, when you proposed, I had no idea they lived so close by."

I'd be lying if I said it didn't bother me that he'd never introduced me to his folks. "No wedding date until I meet the parents," I insisted.

By demanding that, I was able to delay selecting a date. For now.

Rex had heard this before. "You don't understand. My parents aren't like yours."

I nodded. "You've said that at least fifty times, but you've never explained why. Are you embarrassed for them to meet me?"

"No. I'm embarrassed to have *you* meet *them*," Rex said.

"You're an only child like me." I started stacking the wedding magazines. "They're going to want you to be happy."

Rex winced. "I never told you I was an only child."

What? "You have siblings? Why haven't you told me that before?"

"You never asked."

Ah. The old *you-never-asked* trick. I'd used it many times as a spy and a few times as a troop leader. It was an excellent way to lie without truly lying. You just withheld certain intel. It was especially useful when you didn't want the Colombian drug lord you were partying with to know you're a spy. Technically, Carlos the Armadillo *never asked* if I was with the CIA, which meant it was his own fault when he was kidnapped at a convenience store in Bogotá by men in dark suits. He never should've told me about his midnight Slurpee cravings.

"I suppose your sisters or brothers or whatever live in Des Moines too?" I accused.

My fiancé had the good grace to lower his gaze. "Actually, no. They don't live there."

I relented a little. "Fine. I don't know why you hid them from me, but now, before we set a date, I have to meet them too."

"That should be pretty easy." Rex avoided my eyes.

"How's that, if they don't live near your parents?" The city was only thirty minutes away. The only way it would be easier to meet them would be if…

The man I love cleared his throat and suddenly became fascinated with his fingernails. "Because they live here."

CHAPTER THREE

———

After recovering from that bit of news, I grabbed my coat and keys. "Where? We're going to see them right now."

Rex shook his head. "It's not that simple. My sisters and I haven't spoken in years."

"You haven't spoken in years? Why do they live here, then? And why haven't you told me about them before?"

I poured us each a glass of juice. It seemed like the right thing to do.

Rex sat down at the breakfast bar and was again immediately assaulted by the cats. Philby head-butted his arm over and over until he scratched between her ears. I had to give her credit—she knew how to get what she wanted. Martini ran around in circles, pausing every few seconds to fall over with dizziness. She wasn't that bright.

Rex began, "Randi and Ronni are…well, kind of strange."

"Randi and Ronni?" I asked.

He nodded. "Both ending in the letter *i*. Twins. They moved here last month. I just found out."

"Can I call you Rexi?" I asked.

"No." He gave me a threatening look.

"Why don't you get along?" I wanted to add *and again, why didn't you tell me*, but my experience in interrogating told me that would lead to a dead end.

Rex drank his orange juice, as if he was trying to stall. I folded my arms over my chest to let him know he wasn't leaving the house until he told me.

"I'm ten years younger, so I was kind of their baby. They wanted me to be a doctor or lawyer, so when I became a cop, they disapproved." Rex shifted uncomfortably on the stool.

"Also, they're a little unusual," he continued. "My sisters have always been together, and by that, I mean they've never spent one night apart in their entire lives. They dress alike, have the same haircut, and even eat all the same foods. Now they've moved here."

"Why move here? For work?"

"I guess so…"

"What do they do? And if you stall any longer I'm going to get my pliers and car battery with jumper cables."

He looked off into space, weighing his options before giving in. "They're taxidermists. I'm not sure why Who's There seemed like a better option, but before that they lived in What Cheer."

Iowa had a strange history for naming towns. Back in the 1950s, the game show *Truth or Consequences* announced a prize for the first city to take the show's title as their name. A town in New Mexico beat Peterstown, Iowa to it. So the city officials decided to make their own good fortune by naming themselves after another TV show—*Who's There?*—in hopes that the game show would shower us with honors. Unfortunately, the game show got cancelled instead (and had shown no interest whatsoever, anyway), and our name stuck. You'd be hard pressed to find anyone who remembered why we even had this stupid name.

"How did you find out they'd moved here?"

"Officer Dooley pulled Ronni over for speeding. When he submitted the paperwork, I wondered if it was my sister. A little surveillance told me they're hanging out their shingle for taxidermy right here, in town."

Again with Kevin Dooley, the mouth-breather who went to high school with me. He ended up being my lab partner a couple of times, which, in fact, lowered my GPA, probably by osmosis. It was interesting to think of him doing something other than eating junk food or staring blankly into space.

"I don't know which surprises me most," I whistled. "That your sisters moved here or that Kevin handed out an actual ticket and did the paperwork follow-up."

Rex sighed. "You need to cut Officer Dooley some slack."

"You didn't see him eat paste back in the day."

"Kids do that all the time," Rex protested.

"Not in high school." I scooped up my keys. "So, let's go see the twins!"

"I can't." Rex set down his glass. "Another day." He got to his feet and kissed me on the cheek. "I'd better get to work."

He fled my house as if I'd just set the aforementioned car battery and pliers on the table. Of course, I wouldn't do that. They're in the basement—it would take a while to find them.

I grabbed my cell and launched a search for Randi and Ronni Ferguson and taxidermy. Huh. They were working out of the old Peters house across town.

If Who's There had a lame equivalent to the Kennedy family, it was the Peters. In the 1800s, Theobald Peters and his bride Euphemia started this small town with a lumber mill and tavern that quickly became the largest businesses in the county. That's where the similarity to the Kennedys ends.

Dozens had flocked to Peterstown to work in the mill and drink in the tavern. Turns out, a lumber mill and tavern weren't exactly compatible. And since Theobald was a bit of a drinker, the men who worked at the mill usually had "liquid" breakfast at the tavern first. Within a year, we had the largest number of accidental amputees in the whole Midwest.

Euphemia saved the day by taking over the tavern and opening it only after five at night, offering lard sandwiches and charging only half price for the drinks—unofficially creating the first Happy Hour (an important morale booster since half the town had hooks for hands). She also was rumored to have invented a rather unpopular drink called the Cat's Tongue, which consisted of coffee grounds, lard (Euphemia liked lard), and a lot of gin. No one drank this. Ever.

With their success, the Peters built this huge Victorian mansion over on Main Street. It should probably be noted that at the time it was the only house in town because Main Street was the only street in town.

The town sort of grew up around that Victorian house and its businesses. The Peters family lived there until the 1960s, when the last one died in a drowning accident. Since then, the house has been a museum, a shoe store, and very, very briefly, a bordello (which was literally marched on with pitchforks, causing the "employees" to flee into the night). Now, according to my research, it was *Ferguson Taxidermy—Where Your Pet Lives On Forever!*

I checked the hours of operation and realized they'd be open soon. I was going to visit Rex's sisters today. Sisters who would someday be mine! I'd always wanted siblings. Granted, I'd always imagined them to be scientists or artists, but working with animal carcasses would do.

As I got ready, I came up with a cover story, threw on a coat, and headed out. I figured it was too soon to just barge in and introduce myself as their new sister-in-law-to-be. Playing it safe without lying would be the safest route to go.

It took all of four minutes to get there, and that's because traffic was backed up (which meant a farmer had driven a combine into town during rush hour). The old Victorian looked a little run-down but hadn't changed from its original design.

As the largest home in town, my parents used to tell me the king and queen of town lived there. I believed it until kindergarten when I met Kelly, who, in her usual matter-of-fact way, told me I was an idiot and it was just a house. We've been best friends ever since.

"Hello?" I pushed open the door, and a loud gunshot went off.

I dove for the floor and crawled behind a display case.

"I told you, Ronni!" a female voice shouted. "We should just have a *bell*. The sound of a gunshot will scare people!"

"But it's fitting, isn't it?" Another voice that sounded exactly like the first (but angrier) insisted, "We do a lot of animals killed by hunters. A gunshot adds authenticity!"

I popped up behind the display case and brushed myself off. The women weren't startled, which led me to believe this had happened before.

"Hi!" I said brightly. "Welcome to Who's There."

They were completely identical right down to their shoes. Both women were short, like tiny, older versions of Rex. However, there was a distinct difference in their expressions, as one woman looked friendly and the other had a scowl etched into her face.

The woman who smiled grasped my hand introduced herself. "I'm Randi. This is my sister, Ronni. How can we help you?"

Ronni scowled at me. "You live in Iowa. Haven't you heard a gunshot before?"

Of course I had. I was a spy once. "Yes. I just wasn't expecting it."

For a moment I wondered what being an Iowan had to do with it, but then I remembered that on her farm, Grandma Wrath kept a loaded shotgun by the kitchen door. She went her whole life without using it until dementia set in at age ninety-three. After that, she shot at trees for reasons no one could understand, until she had a stroke a year later. At her funeral, we had memorials made out to the Arbor Foundation. It seemed like the right thing to do after Grandma's yearlong tree assassinations.

Randi beamed. Ronni narrowed her angry eyes. They were twins in everything but temperament. Unable to figure out what to say next, I studied the room. From all angles, high above me, badgers, squirrels, deer heads, coyotes, hawks, and a skunk dressed as a clown glared down at me. I backed into a giant buck wearing a raincoat and tripped over what appeared to be a dinner party scene with garter snakes.

"The skunk is for sale." Randi smiled. "The others are special orders. Did you want to buy something?"

For a moment, I toyed with asking if I could outbid whoever ordered the snake party but decided I didn't want to start off our new relationship with a disagreement. My cover story poked me in the brain.

"Sure. I was looking for something unique to give to a friend. She loves dead animals."

"I've got some interesting things in the next room," Randi (who didn't seem to think this was a strange thing for someone to love) said as she motioned for me to follow her.

Ronni crossed her arms over her chest. I think she even growled at me as I squeezed past her. That woman's stare would wilt flowers. I'd never met someone so unpleasant. Well, that's not entirely true. There was this monsignor in Paraguay with halitosis and Tourette syndrome who hated me because my first name started with the letter *F*. Considering that his name was Father Farquard, I assumed he was just being difficult.

With the twins, my strategy would be to befriend Randi and hope someday Ronni would come around.

"Here!" Randi handed me a dead kitten. "She's holding a little doll!"

The white kitten had blue eyes and was dressed as a little girl with a hair bow, pink dress, and tiny doll. It was disturbing, especially considering I had two live cats at home—who would never forgive me if I bought this.

"She's allergic to cats," I said about my fake friend who didn't exist.

"Oh! Well…" Randi turned to an open display cabinet filled with small animals in various clothing, pretending to be humans. "How about this?" she asked as she handed me something.

It was an armadillo with a ukulele.

"They're very big in Japan!"

Where did they get an armadillo in Iowa? I pushed that thought from my mind as I declined.

"Are you going to buy something or what?" Ronni glowered from the doorway. "I hate looky-loos. People should only come in here if they're serious about buying something."

"Why don't you go finish the squirrel Phantom of the Opera diorama?" Randi said calmly to her sister. "The client is picking it up tomorrow."

Ronni muttered a few words I couldn't hear before disappearing. The room seemed to brighten in her absence.

"How about that?" I pointed to a large crow wearing a Groucho nose, mustache, and glasses. He appeared to be in the middle of a stand-up act, with a microphone clutched in his right claw and a rubber chicken next to his other foot.

Randi beamed. "That's Sigurd! An excellent choice!"

I thought so. With the fake glasses, I couldn't see his beady eyes much. Maybe the cats would like it. Or I could give it to Finn, my infant goddaughter and Kelly's baby…if babies liked that sort of thing. I really wasn't sure.

Randi plucked the dead bird from the case and took it back to the front, where she began to wrap it in blaze orange and green camouflage tissue paper.

"How long have you been in town?" I asked as casually as I could for someone buying a dead crow impersonating a stand-up comic.

"Oh, just a month." Randi's tongue stuck out to the side as she very gingerly stuffed tissue paper into the crevices around the bird.

"What made you move here?" I asked.

"We fell in love with this house." She smiled. The woman seemed very sweet. Rex must have been exaggerating.

"So, you'd been here before?" I asked.

"That's right." Randi finished wrapping the paper around the thing before tucking him into a paper bag with handles. "There you go! That's two hundred dollars."

Two hundred dollars? I could shoot a bird in my yard for less than that. But I handed over the money anyway, hoping the look on my face indicated that I did this kind of thing every day.

"Do you know anyone in town?" I pressed as she handed me the bag.

"Oh yes." She beamed. "We have a brother who lives here."

Aha!

Ronni screamed from the other room, "Why aren't you gone yet? People have work to do, you know!"

Time to go. "Well thank you," I said as I backed toward the door. "I hope your business does well here!" This time I flinched only a little when the gunshot doorbell went off.

Back at home a few minutes later, I opened the bag and plopped Sigurd down in front of the cats. Philby's tail twitched as she walked around the thing, hissing at odd moments. After completing her circuit, she punched the bird in its fake nose. When the inanimate crow didn't flee in the face of her fury, Philby lost interest and walked away.

Martini hunkered down before taking a run at it. When the crow didn't move, she seemed disappointed and settled for munching on his tail feathers.

I snatched Sigurd from her. "This isn't for you." I put the bird on the fridge where I thought he might be safe.

Rex didn't seem to appreciate the gift a few hours later when I took it over to his office.

"You went to see my sisters, didn't you?" His eyes were riveted on the dead beast on his desk.

I pulled up a chair. "I was sitting there this morning, thinking *Rexi needs something in his office, but what?* And that's when I realized you needed this guy. His name is Sigurd."

He shoved the bird aside. "Why did you go?"

"Why haven't *you* gone there?" I shot back.

"I haven't seen my sisters in years," he countered. Rex was adorable when he verbally sparred with me.

"Why haven't you seen your sisters in years?" I asked. "If I had sisters, I'd visit them every week. Maybe more often." That was true. I didn't really like being an only child.

Rex seemed to know he was outgunned. He pushed back in his chair. "Just don't go back."

I shook my head. "I'm thinking of going back there every day and buying something for your office until you introduce me properly."

He sent me home with Sigurd.

Fine. I'd break into his house in the middle of the night and put Sigurd on his nightstand. That would show him. Maybe a judgy dead animal with a sense of humor would change his mind about his family.

After several hours of trying Sigurd out in different spots around the house, I settled him in my bedroom on top of a tall wardrobe. The cats wouldn't be able to get him there, but I'd have to remember where I'd put him so I didn't freak out in the night about shadows of birds attacking me.

Lying down on the bed to get a better perspective, I felt woozy. Closing my eyes, I thought for about a second about Rex's sisters. And then, I fell asleep.

It was dark when I woke up. Whoa. How long had I been out? After a nod to the dead crow, I headed to the kitchen to give the cats their supper, where I found Rex sitting at the breakfast bar, reading the newspaper. This was significant because I didn't subscribe to the newspaper.

"I forgot to mention earlier, Officer Dooley searched the Fontanas' house last night," he said without looking up.

I fed the cats and poured myself a bowl of Lucky Charms, adding extra marshmallows. I'd discovered this particular cereal during a campout with my troop. Kelly was not happy when I had four bowls in a row. She said I was bad at sharing.

My fiancé was a bit of a foodie, and while he'd never directly disparaged my childish eating habits, he'd made it clear that he'd do the cooking once we were wed.

The thought caused flutters in my stomach.

"He didn't find anything. No body and nothing out of order."

"You sent an idiot to do a real cop's job," I grumbled as I poured milk over the cereal.

Rex set the paper down. "Officer Dooley is a real cop. You need to stop giving him a hard time."

I pointed my spoon at him. "Tell me one thing he's good at. Then I'll leave him alone."

Rex stared thoughtfully into space before saying, "He's great at ordering lunch for the station, and he's actually pretty good at paperwork."

"I'm not sure those count." I stirred my cereal until all the rainbow colors bled into the milk.

"Fortunately for you and to my surprise"—Rex nodded toward my neighbors' house—"the Fontanas are not angry and didn't complain. If they had, I'd have had to come over and give you a good talking to."

With a mouthful of marshmallows, I managed, "That would be okay if by *a talking to* you mean making out over a bucket of fried chicken with an Oreo chaser."

Rex laughed and got to his feet. He kissed me on the forehead, since I was mid-chew, and told me he had to head home and get some sleep.

"Try not to spy on the neighbors tonight. I'd like a full night's sleep."

And with that, he walked out the door.

CHAPTER FOUR

I wiggled my eyebrows at Philby. "We know what we saw—don't we, girl?"

The fact that the neighbors weren't in the least upset that I'd sent the police to their house in the middle of the night was curious. I'd be outraged. Why weren't they?

It wasn't too late, so I grabbed my keys and ran to the hardware store to buy some binoculars. Even though my neighbors were…well…neighbors, I needed to be able to see everything.

I loved this store. All of the employees were little old men in overalls who knew where every screw and washer was located on a wall full of thousands of little drawers. Of course, binoculars were easier to find, as they were by the front door. Within minutes, I had what I needed.

I was just congratulating myself for being clever, when I turned the ignition in my car and a man jumped in on the passenger side.

Without thinking, and acting reflexively, I punched him in the throat.

The man gasped and, in a gravelly voice as he faced me, croaked out, "Hey! Easy now!"

"Riley? What are you doing here? And why are you in my car? And why are you in disguise?"

Riley Andrews, my former handler and one-time boyfriend, had a thick red mullet, sported a five o'clock shadow, and was wearing a shirt with the sleeves torn off. He looked like my mechanic, come to think of it. This was a departure from his usual tailored suits, permanent tan, and thick, longish, wavy blond hair.

He studied my face. "Wow, Wrath, you look like you haven't slept in a month." *The bastard.*

I pointed at his wig. "You look like my mechanic, Stewie."

Riley tugged on his wig. "That sounds promising."

"Stewie doesn't have any teeth, and in the last presidential election, he wrote BALLS as a write-in candidate." True story. I've only seen him once in the last two years, but he was good with cars. "What are you doing here?"

Due to circumstances of his own making, Riley had left the CIA. I'd heard rumors through the grapevine that he'd since joined the FBI. Which, in our line of work, is like American troops going over to the Nazi side.

Just to be clear, Riley didn't work or live here. And since my engagement he'd been sending me mixed messages on how he feels about me. So, punching him in the throat was completely justified.

"Just passing through." He winked. "I'm working on something. I was just in Omaha and am heading to Chicago."

"You couldn't fly between the two cities?"

It occurred to me I might be hallucinating. Riley in a mullet was just too ridiculous to be real. I pinched him for good measure. He flinched. He was real.

"And miss seeing you looking like a zombie? No way."

I ignored the crack. "So, it's true. You're a Fed now."

He nodded. "It took months to clean up the mess I'd made with the Agency. They decided to kick me out. The FBI practically recruited me on the spot."

"You've gone to the dark side," I warned. "I don't know if I can be seen in public with you anymore."

"Face it, Wrath." He leaned dangerously close. "You'll miss me too much."

I was going to tell him about the Fontanas and their dead body, but his comment changed my mind.

I shoved him back against the door. "You'd better get going. You've got about a five-hour drive ahead of you."

He shrugged. "There's no hurry. I could stick around for a couple of days if you want."

"I don't want," I mumbled, sounding like a toddler. "How did you know I was here?"

Riley smiled a smile I hadn't seen in a while. It was closed and suggestive and sneaky.

"I was driving around and saw your van."

My van was silver with generic plates. There had to be twenty or thirty silver minivans in town.

"You were spying on me," I said after a moment.

He gave me a measured look I couldn't interpret. What was he up to, and what did it have to do with me?

"I was not spying on you," he insisted at long last. "I was driving down Main Street and saw you walking out of this shop."

It was possible he was telling the truth about seeing me. I'd been so sleep deprived, I could've missed spotting him. On the other hand, he'd been a spy. You couldn't trust spies to stop spying. And yes, I know that applies to me too. And yes, I was completely guilty on that count.

"Go to Chicago, Riley." I sighed.

"Your loss, Wrath," Riley said as he got out of my car and climbed into his own.

The man was gorgeous. With his perennial tan, startling blue eyes, and thick, wavy blond hair, he could melt the panties off many women—and did. His charm was off the charts, and he had a body like Adonis.

And I needed him out of my life. Yet somehow, when I least expected it, Riley always knew how to show up and toss a wrench into the works. What was it about him that made me crazy?

As he drove off, I stifled a yawn. I needed to go home and go to bed. Lately, the insomnia pounded through my brain, flooding it with all kinds of thoughts, from my fear about the wedding, to my troop, to the great unanswered questions in life. Like, why isn't a group of squid called a squad? Why do people consider meatloaf a comfort food? If the plural of *ox* is *oxen*—why isn't the plural of *fox*, *foxen*?

The things that kept me up at night demonstrated that I might be certifiable.

Back at home, Philby and Martini were nowhere to be found. I guess they weren't taking their assignment of watching the Fontanas seriously. Oh well. I might as well get some sleep. I stripped out of my clothes and climbed into bed. A minute later I felt two cats jump onto the bed and snuggle up against me. Their purring was the perfect thing to lure me to sleep.

The strangest dream played out in my head. The Fontanas were carrying a body, in broad daylight, into the house. It was me. And I was in some sort of coma that meant I could see and hear but couldn't move or speak.

Once inside the house, they carried me to a large coffin where Philby waited with a nail and a hammer, making meaningful eye contact.

"*Noooooooooo!*" I sat up, covered in sweat. The cats didn't stir or even look at me. Did I do this a lot? The clock on my nightstand said it was two in the afternoon.

I'd slept! Yay! I actually got some sleep! Hey! How did I sleep from last night through to this afternoon? And why did I still feel so tired?

My cell buzzed from the pillow next to me. It was a text from Kelly. I was late for a troop meeting that started now. Uh-oh.

The school where we met regularly was at the other end of the block, so it only took me a few minutes to get there. I stopped in the doorway, panting heavily. Every pair of eyes in the room turned toward me.

"You're late, Mrs. Wrath!" Emily accused, pointing a finger at me as if she'd just discovered I was a pod clone. I half expected her to hiss.

For the eight billionth time in two years, I said, "It's *Ms.*, Emily."

I don't know why I corrected them. The girl labored under the delusion that I was old, and therefore, like all old women, a *Mrs*. Nothing I could do or say ever changed this.

"As I was saying, ladies..." Kelly, my best friend and co-leader, narrowed her eyes at me before turning back to the girls. "World Thinking Day is only a few weeks away, and we still haven't picked a country."

Oh. Right. The Thinking Day thing. We did a booth every year. Normally the event was in February, but the arena where these things were held had mysteriously caught fire last month and the whole thing was put off until late March. This was good because we'd originally had a scheduling conflict with the event, as I'd booked a winter campout. Because of the fire, we were able to go camping *and* participate in Thinking Day.

The campout had been fun, but Kelly thought my presentation on winter camouflage for snipers was a tad too much. The girls had loved it, and for our craft project, we'd made white ghillie suits using toilet paper. By the way—toilet paper disintegrates in snow—but sometimes you just had to work with what's at hand at the moment.

The girls shouted out various countries from France to Fiji, with a brief debate when Inez brought up North Korea.

"It's been in the news a lot," the girl said.

Betty, not usually the moral compass of the group, shrieked, "We can't do North Korea! It's run by a megalomaniac despot! Besides, we know nothing of their real culture because all information is pure propaganda."

My mouth dropped open, and she shrugged.

"What? I read it in *Foreign Affairs* magazine."

Betty was well on her way to a bright career in the CIA. I wondered if I could put in a recommendation now. Maybe since she was in my troop, they'd consider her a legacy.

Inez stared menacingly as she folded her arms over her chest—a move that meant either she was very angry or we were very stupid. Many times they meant the same thing.

"Somebody has to have been there because it is a place with people," the girl snapped.

I'd been to North Korea. Briefly. Very briefly on assignment. Riley and I had barely made it out alive. I can't give you the details because it's classified…but it involved an avocado, a feral penguin, and three feet of rope.

"What about Spain?" Lauren asked.

Betty shook her head. "We shouldn't do Spain until they allow Catalonia its own government."

I was pretty certain Spain wouldn't see our boycott in Who's There, Iowa and think, *Hey! Maybe those little girls in the middle of nowhere are right! We should totally grant Catalonia their independence! Why didn't we think of that? Thanks, little girls in the middle of nowhere!*

"Merry! Focus," Kelly whispered, and I realized I'd been absentmindedly flamenco dancing.

I cleared my throat. "How about France? Didn't someone say France?"

Four little girls stepped forward and nodded. The Kaitlyns. I had four Kaitlyns. All with the letter *M* as the initial for their last names. And all with mothers named Ashley. Sometimes I wondered if I was living in an alternate universe.

"Okay! France, it is," I agreed.

"But what about the Basque people?" Betty complained.

"And the treachery of the Vichy French?" Caterina, normally the quietest kid in the troop, nodded. "I can't be the only one here who hasn't forgiven them for that."

Every pair of eyes turned to her.

She shrugged. "What? I watch a lot of the *History Channel.*"

The girls broke into a hot political debate about the flaws and defects of European countries of the Iberian Peninsula.

"This is all your fault." My co-leader sighed.

Of course she blamed me. "Me? How is this my fault?"

She threw up her arms. "You had to give them all a copy of the CIA's *World Factbook* for Christmas."

"Hey! I got a great deal from the Government Printing Office."

This guy I know there had owed me a favor because I scored him a case of Girl Scout cookies out of season. Since when is it a bad idea to give the gift of education? And, do you know how hard it is to get hold of a case of Thin Mints in November? That's three whole months before orders even start. I had to call in a couple of favors from two Uzbeks (former moles I helped with US Visas) in Chicago who knew a guy, who knew a lady who ran one of the bakeries. You may not realize it, but that action was trickier than wet work in Ecuador. Unless it's monsoon season, that is.

Kelly held up the signal for the quiet sign—one of my favorite things in scouting. The girls went back to their seats and looked at her expectantly. I was convinced that someday this could be used for world peace. Well, at least peace between Iceland and Greenland. It's a little known fact that those two do *not* like each other.

"We'll do France," my co-leader said.

Caterina and Betty started to protest, but she held up the quiet sign again and the girls stopped speaking.

"Let's keep it simple, shall we?" Kelly said. "We can make chocolate éclairs"—this got the girls' attention—"play French music, and wear berets…"

Betty grumbled, "Berets are from the Basque Country."

"Well," Kelly said quickly, "most people think they are French, so we will just go with that."

"Good call," I leaned in and whispered.

Kelly nodded at me and turned to the kids. "Let's get on the computers in here and see what all we can find out about French culture."

We spent the next hour and a half printing off pictures and gluing them onto a huge piece of poster board. Kelly was really into collaging. By the end of the meeting, we had a mushy, wet mess of pictures of everything from croissants to the Eiffel Tower. At some point Betty slapped on a sign that said *Freedom for Basque Country*, but Kelly removed it.

I really admired the woman, even if she could be a wet blanket. My best friend since we were in elementary school ourselves, Kelly was everything a leader should be—organized, good at paperwork, and smart. I was the one who got dirty, hid dead terrorists in the low-ropes course, and binged on the dozens of s'mores the girls made for us.

I was lucky to have her. She even named Riley and me as her daughter's godparents. I didn't quite know what that meant or what my job description was. I do know it doesn't mean the baby is supposed to treat us like gods (an idea that led Kelly to sigh and roll her eyes).

One of the moms stuck her head inside the door, and I realized the meeting had ended ten minutes ago. This was unusual because our parents were so inactive they were almost invisible. Most of the time they sat in their cars, staring at their cells until their daughters jumped into the car, reminding them that they had a kid.

"…and I was thinking we could all do pink T-shirts, black leggings, and ballet flats." Kelly was speaking to me because there wasn't anyone else in the room. The girls had all gone.

I snapped back to the present. "Great idea! I'll order the berets."

"There's something else." Kelly handed me a newspaper article.

It was about a king vulture on loan to the local zoo from the Smithsonian in Washington DC. After a trip there, my girls had met and named him Mr. Fancy Pants.

"He's here?" I gasped. "Already?"

The picture in the black and white paper didn't do him justice. With a brilliant purple and black head covered in stubble, the bird had a brightly colored wattle over his beak and two eyes that seemed to move independently from each other. They looked like googly eyes, giving the bird a slightly deranged, muppety kind of look.

Kelly nodded and took the article back. "I talked to the zoo. They know about our history with the bird and are going to let us visit in a few days. I'm waiting for confirmation but wanted to give you a heads-up before I told the girls."

"What are we going to do on this visit?" I thought about the bird and how he'd once helped me catch a member of the Yakuza. Also, he was heavily addicted to Girl Scout cookies. Shortbread was his favorite, if I remembered correctly.

"Nothing. We'll just have a simple visit." From her expression, I could see she hadn't thought that far.

"Okay. I'll pull some cookies from the freezer." *Be prepared* was the Girl Scout motto, after all.

My co-leader looked doubtful. "Didn't you say he attacks for cookies? That might not be a good idea."

I shrugged. "It seems rude not to take them. Kind of like how you told me I should take wine to that party last month."

Kelly and I had been invited to a party hosted by a nurse she worked with. Originally, I was going to give the host lanyards made by the girls. Who doesn't love handcrafts made from plastic laces? (According to Kelly, everybody). I should've known because each country is different. In Morocco, you bring milk or yogurt. In China they like fruit, and you have to bring two pieces—but never pears, for reasons I don't understand. And chocolate works as a gift in almost every country, but I couldn't figure out how to keep s'mores hot on the way there.

Like my friend suggested, I'd taken wine, and everything seemed okay. That is, until we discovered that the host was allergic to the tannins in red wine (something she didn't know about herself). Fortunately, there'd been lots of nurses and doctors on hand to deal with it. I'd gotten the impression that my co-leader thought I was to blame somehow. She didn't say so, but my instinct had told that was the case. After all, I'd done what she'd suggested. How could she be mad at that?

Kelly thought for a moment. "I'm looking forward to meeting Fancy Pants."

"Mr. Fancy Pants," I corrected.

I thought about the bird's impending visit as I walked home. My stomach rumbled, making me realize I'd missed lunch. I didn't like missing meals. And all that talk about cookies had made me hungry. We'd just finished selling Girl Scout cookies, and I had three cases of them in my basement. All I needed was a huge glass of milk, and I'd have a well-balanced lunch.

As I neared my house, the hairs went up on the back of my neck. Someone was watching me. I kept moving as if nothing was off and noticed that the man my fiancé called Mark Fontana was standing in his driveway, staring at me. There was no car present. He was just standing there with nothing in his hands, blatantly watching me.

"Hi!" I called out cheerfully, and walked over with my hand out. "I'm Merry Wrath. I don't think we've met."

Fontana looked like every other generic thirty-something male whose face would be forgotten moments after meeting him. He was my height, slightly plump, with a receding hairline and a hair color I'd call browneige. He was sporting a white polo shirt and jeans that seemed to make him bland and invisible as he stared at me strangely.

Probably because he knew I'd called the cops on him for carrying a dead body the other night. And while Rex insisted there was no evidence of this, I knew what I'd seen. Philby'd seen it too, so I know I hadn't been hallucinating.

The man shook my hand and said at last, "I'm glad we're finally meeting. Rex is your fiancé, right?" He nodded to the house across the street.

"That's right. He's only lived here a couple of years, but I grew up here. You and your wife?"

"We're from Minneapolis." He smiled at last. "Before that we were from Canada. Met at the University of Iowa."

That seemed like an odd bit of information to volunteer. Something about this guy seemed off *and* completely normal, all at the same time. I just couldn't figure out if I was smart or paranoid. There's a fine line there, believe it or not.

"Are those your cats?" Mark pointed at my front window where the two felines were sitting, staring at us.

"Yeah. Philby's on the left, and that's Martini on the right. You wouldn't have met them. They aren't outside cats."

He squinted. "Am I seeing things, or does Philby look like Hitler?"

I nodded. "She does. It's kind of hard to miss, isn't it?" Hopefully this guy wasn't a Nazi as well as a conveyor of dead bodies.

Mark looked uneasy. "Sorry for just blurting that out. You don't see that every day."

"Do you and your wife have any pets?" Small talk 101—bring up pets and kids to disarm people.

Mark shook his head. "Good God, no! I'm not much of a pet person."

Who wasn't a pet person? I wasn't sure I wanted a neighbor who wasn't a pet person.

"So, Mark, what do you do?" Small talk 102—move on to occupations. It only works in America—where for some reason the citizens judge each other by their jobs. In other countries, ask about anything else, like the weather or the fetishes of the current dictator.

"My wife and I...Pam, we have an insurance company. We're not affiliated with any one provider. We're more like middlemen."

"Here in Who's There?" I thought about this for a moment. "Insurance United? In the strip mall on the outskirts of town?" It was the only insurance company I knew.

My neighbor nodded. "That's right. We bought it from the Turners when they retired."

"That's interesting." Now, why does someone move to a tiny town in the middle of nowhere for no real reason? I added this to my mental list of suspicious activities.

"What do you do, Merry?" Mark asked.

I couldn't very well tell him I'd been a spy. It had been a closely held secret, one I was sure would get out by the time of my wedding, when Senator and Mrs. Czrygy arrived in town for the ceremony.

"I'm between jobs right now." Not a lie! "I mostly volunteer up at the school with a Girl Scout troop."

"That's good to know," he said cryptically. "Well, I should get inside. Pam's making Yankee pot roast and apple pie for dinner. We love American food!" He stuck out his hand and shook mine again. "It was nice to meet you. Maybe we can go out to dinner, Pam and me and you and Rex?"

"Sure," I answered. "Nice meeting you too."

Once I got inside the house, I pulled some pizza rolls and ranch dressing out of the fridge and thought about my neighbors. Like Rex thought, Mark seemed normal and nice. Not like a killer at all. Of course, you can't count on a first meeting to sum up a person's character. I learned that lesson the hard way with a Tibetan prince and priest in the Galapagos. Turned out the "man of the cloth" was an iguana smuggler. And, an actual prince.

"I know we saw something the other night," I said to Philby, who'd jumped onto the counter. "Didn't we?"

Philby turned around in circles three times before sitting her ample butt down.

"That's a yes, right?" I opened a couple of cans of cat food and was joined by Martini.

None of this answered my question. But it did add to my doubts. In spite of my recent success with the nap earlier, I was tired. I hadn't slept through the night in a while, and even though I hadn't dreamed it, I guess it's possible that I maybe, might have hallucinated.

Mark seemed okay and didn't appear to be upset that I'd called the police on him. Maybe I should just give him the benefit of the doubt.

I rubbed my face. If I could just get some real sleep. My eyes settled on the stack of bridal magazines on the breakfast bar, and I felt a spike in blood pressure.

Thinking of the wedding made my heart race and my palms sweat. It was definitely one of the factors that kept me up all those nights. I wasn't sure why. I loved Rex and was sure we'd be happy together.

There were just too many questions. Would I be able to live with someone after so many years on my own? Would I miss being able to come and go as I chose without checking in with someone? Would I be able to give up my house? Did I want to take his last name?

And then there was Riley. He wasn't trying to break us up, exactly, but there was a vibe I couldn't ignore. I wasn't sure if I still had feelings for him or if I was irritated because he was throwing me off.

How was this going to work, anyway? Rex and I didn't even spend every day together. We saw each other quite a bit and always had dates on the weekends. But how was this going to work living in the same house? Would we love it or get on each other's nerves? I had no idea what to expect. And was that normal?

What I did know was that I'd been thinking so long it was now dark outside. For some reason I was wondering about Mark and Pam's marriage. I hadn't met her, but it sounded like they'd been together for a while. I mean, she was making pot roast and pie for dinner. That sounded normal. As American as apple pie, so they say.

Maybe I could study them. Find out what made their marriage tick. Sure, I had Kelly and Robert and my parents, but I needed a fresh look at things. As I did the dishes, I made up my mind to begin Operation Fontana as soon as I could figure out how to launch it.

At this point it was spring, and I'd gotten engaged in the fall. Guilt crept into my brain. I needed to start taking some steps toward making this wedding happen. If I did that, maybe I'd be able to sleep like a normal human.

And to pull off that miracle, I'd need my mother.

CHAPTER FIVE

————

"Darling!" Judith Czrygy's voice bubbled through the phone ten minutes later. "How are the plans for your nuptials coming along?"

See? That's why I needed her! I didn't even know about the word *nuptials*. Which meant there was a lot I didn't know. I'd gone to the right woman.

A flicking tail caught my eye, and since I have the attention span of a gnat, I looked. Philby was plastered (legs splayed, belly and nose smooshed against the glass as if she'd been shot in the back) to the front window, staring at Rex's house. She'd been banned due to a mouse infestation months ago.

Rex had had the exterminators over three times and was finally declared mouse-free. He said he wanted to wait to bring the cats over until he knew it was safe for them. Philby's nose pressed so hard against the glass I was afraid it would break. She couldn't understand why all that fun killing of little furry things had stopped. It was a little sad.

And then I realized I was still on the phone. "I'm hitting a snag, Mom. I was thinking maybe you could come down for a few days to help?"

It sounded like my mom was dancing with glee. I thought I'd even heard a champagne cork fly in the background.

"Of course! I'll make the flight arrangements and hopefully see you tomorrow!"

"Tomorrow?" I must've said aloud.

Mom quickly piped up. "I'll only stay a couple of days, and I'll make reservations at the Radisson."

"You could stay here," I mumbled. I regretted it as soon as I said it, since due to a misunderstanding a little while back, there were bullet holes all over my guest room.

"Absolutely not." I could swear she was shaking her head. "Rex texted me that you were having trouble sleeping. I don't want to make it worse. I'll just stay long enough to get the ball rolling, and then I'll head back to DC. Deal?"

Like I could say no to that.

Lying in bed that night, I tossed and turned. Sleep was still evading me, and I was very frustrated. Finally I got out of bed at 1 a.m. and headed into the kitchen. Philby was waiting for me, as if she knew all along I'd be there.

"Oh," I snapped, "like you've got it all figured out."

Philby looked at me to indicate that my accusation was beneath her. Then she walked over to the door to the garage and sat, facing it.

That was odd. She never wanted out. Philby was averse to cold, rain, and the whole outdoors in general. She'd only been in the garage once before, and that was the other night. And yet, here she was, trying to tell me she wanted back in there.

"Do we have mice?" I wondered aloud.

Maybe I had mice too. There was one way to check. I opened the door and turned on the light. Philby was back in the windowsill and hissed at me until I turned the light off. What was she up to?

I joined her in the window. Not because I was paranoid about the neighbors, but because clearly my cat had a problem and it would be good for me to find out what was going on so I could help her.

Lights were on at the Fontana house. Now, I totally understand that this is normal. Some people are just night owls. I was attacked by an owl at night once, in Estonia. It wasn't pleasant.

Mark and Pam were facing each other, arguing. With two closed windows between us, I caught the tone but not the words. They were throwing their arms around a lot. That was a dead giveaway.

I watched with my cat for a while as the two gesticulated wildly. If I hadn't been a spy, I might've thought watching them was wrong. But I'd made my career watching people surreptitiously. Would Rex put an end to that once we were married?

Philby's eyes were locked on to the couple, tail twitching violently. What was it about the Fontanas that set her off?

I got my answer seconds later when Pam produced a sniper rifle, waving it around in the air. Whoa. It was a Mosin-Nagant. An antique at best. Russian made. Were they collectors? Mark took the weapon from her and disappeared, reappearing seconds later with a hatchet.

He made a chopping motion with it, and she nodded in agreement. What kind of argument starts with a sniper rifle and ends with a hatchet?

"Should we call Rex?" I whispered to my cat.

Philby leveled a gaze at me and belched before turning her attention back to the window.

"I'll take that as a no?"

When I looked back out the window, the Fontanas were now physically fighting. Punches were being thrown—kicks were hitting their mark. I gripped my cell, prepared to call 9-1-1, when it dawned on me. They weren't fighting. They were sparring.

Blows never fully landed as no contact was made between them. My mind justified it with the idea they were into that sort of thing…whatever that sort of thing was. Did couples do this in the middle of the night?

If so, I could get into it. Rex had his police training, and I had my spy training in hand-to-hand combat. That might be fun. It would also keep me sharp.

But these two were insurance agents…with a sniper rifle, hatchet, and fighting skills. What did it mean?

CHAPTER SIX

———

I'm not too proud to say that Philby and I watched them for a few more hours. It was better than television, to tell the truth, and my cat and I had several in-depth and meaningful conversations.

For example, Philby thinks Riley is messing with me, I should marry Rex, and she should have fresh salmon every day. I think there was also an agreement for me to let a mouse loose in the house for her now and then, but I might have imagined that.

Just before dawn, the couple called it quits and turned out the lights. Philby and I went to bed. My mind was racing, and while I think I did sleep for a few moments here and there, at seven in the morning I gave up.

The bathroom mirror told me that the dark circles under my eyes had dark circles of their own, and my skin had taken on a kind of beige/grayish appearance. I decided to call the color greige.

After pouring orange juice on my cereal and milk in my juice glass four times, I gave up. Toast seemed simpler until I put jelly on the stick of butter in the dish. I ate the toast dry.

My cell buzzed with a text from my mother. She was in Chicago but would be landing in Des Moines within the hour. This news jolted me awake, and I changed my clothes and made for the van.

"Mom!" I wheezed over several heads at the baggage claim area after racing through the terminal. I really needed to get into shape. Especially before the wedding. Not that I was out of shape. I was a solid size six. My problem was in running or even walking fast. And while I didn't think the bride usually speed-walked up the aisle, I should start taking strolls at night through the neighborhood, just to get healthier.

Judith Czrygy waved a perfectly manicured hand at me. She didn't look like a woman who'd gotten up early and flown halfway across the country. My beautiful mother was elegant beyond her years. In her late 50s, she looked at least fifteen years younger. Her glossy, honey-gold hair framed her face in silky waves. She was dressed in a cream-colored suit with matching turtleneck. In fact, she looked like an ad in a magazine. This woman was the reason I was insecure about my looks.

Actually, that thought would horrify her because she would never want me to feel bad. But growing up with a mother who was stylish and charming 24/7 wasn't easy. I looked down at my jeans, tennis shoes, and sweatshirt. I hadn't had any time to put on makeup or even brush my hair. I did brush my teeth. I'm not a total loser.

You would've thought I was dressed for prom, the way Mom ran over and hugged me. She was the quintessential DC politician's wife. Even here in the middle of Iowa.

"Your bags?" I asked.

"I'll get them." She handed me an expensive but simple black leather tote bag that doubled as her purse.

"*I'll* get them," I insisted as I shouldered the bag and headed for the conveyor belt.

Mom followed and pointed out her suitcase. I snagged it, and we headed for the parking lot.

"I haven't been back to Who's There since the last campaign," she murmured. "Your father usually travels to Des Moines to meet with constituents, but I rarely leave DC."

"Well, it hasn't changed much." Except for all the murders and the taxidermy shop run by twins.

If my mother thought it was strange for me to own a minivan, she didn't say so. "Thank you for calling me, kiddo. I really needed to get out of town."

I looked at her. "I thought you loved it there."

She shook her head. "I need a break from all the fundraisers and cocktail parties. This is perfect, and I get to meet Philby and Martini. Now, about the wedding—how far have you gotten in the planning?"

"Um, I've got a stack of magazines…"

Mom laughed, and it sounded like the gentle tinkling of wind chimes. "It's a good thing I'm here."

We chatted about foreign things like pew bows and bridesmaid dresses and bouquets as I drove home. Mom threw out phrases that seemed to come from another language. Boutonnieres? Something blue? Canapés? Pew bows? What did it all mean? Maybe I should've cracked open one or two of the wedding magazines before now.

"I'm glad you're handling things." I was reeling. "Rex will be so happy to see you. He thinks I'm not taking this seriously."

Mom arched her right eyebrow. "Are you?"

I shrugged. "I guess not after hearing about *boutonnieres*. Besides, you've planned galas in DC. Dinner parties with heads of state. You'll be perfect."

"Well, let's get started. What's the date?"

I gulped. "I kind of don't have one yet?"

She nodded. "Don't worry. We will figure this out. Let's start at the beginning. What season do you think of when you think of getting married?"

I thought about this for a moment. "I guess I'd like to do it in the winter. I went to a wedding once in December. With the snow and the twinkling stars, it was pretty."

"Good. See? We're getting somewhere! How about mid-December? It'll be between the holidays; the church will be decorated beautifully, and you'll have about eight months to prepare."

It felt like a huge weight had been lifted off my shoulders. "Huh. I hadn't thought of that. It sounds perfect, really."

My mother consulted her cell phone. "Now that we've narrowed it down to the middle of the month, we have two Saturdays to choose from."

She'd just narrowed the possible dates from fifty-two to two! Why didn't I think of that?

"I can't believe it!" Rex met us at the house. "You've accomplished more in thirty minutes than Merry has in one month!"

Rex gave me one of his private little grins. I loved that. It was like our own, special language. Sure, other people could see it, but they didn't know what he was thinking. Okay, *I* didn't know what he was thinking, but I could guess, and I liked what I was guessing.

What did I ever do to deserve this man? Ridiculously handsome and oozing smarts, Rex was a serious catch. Granted, I'd never ask this question out loud because some other woman might overhear and make a play for him.

But Rex was a one-woman man. And that lucky woman was me.

Mom gave Rex a warm hug.

"Where are your bags?" he asked.

"Mom's staying at the Radisson," I said. "We just checked her in, but she wanted to see my house."

Philby and Martini were plastered to the front window, staring at Mom as if she was a giant mouse come to taunt them from across the street.

"The cats!" Mom shouted with glee. "They are so cute!"

I barely got the door open before Philby and Martini knocked me aside and started rubbing up against my mother like teenage girls grinding at the homecoming dance. I ran back to my room to quickly make the bed and returned to find my sophisticated mother, in her expensive wool suit, sitting cross-legged on the floor—her lap filled with cats that looked like Hitler and Elvis.

Philby had joined my household almost two years ago, accompanied by a corpse. She was a great cat but had one weird peccadillo. She hissed violently whenever she heard the name "Bob." For a second I entertained the idea of showing Mom this trick—but decided against it. I saved that little treasure for punishing the cat for vomiting in my slippers or shredding my pillow. If you think I'm teasing, I think it's only fair to tell you I have five destroyed pillows in my closet and am on my fifth pair of slippers this month. Turned out she was pregnant. And that's how I got Martini.

"I have to get back to work." Rex sounded sorry. "I'd love to take you ladies out to dinner tonight."

We agreed, and my fiancé left. One minute later the doorbell rang, and I opened it to find Kelly and her baby, my goddaughter, Finn. This time Mom squealed with glee as she took the baby out of Kelly's arms. Which spiked a real concern that children were expected soon after we tied the knot. I knew I wasn't ready for that.

Kelly and Mom chatted as my best friend caught her up on her parents, husband, and job. Finn was fascinated with my mother, as if she was staring at a huge ice cream sundae. Or whatever babies fantasize about. It should be ice cream. Everybody likes ice cream.

I totally understood the kid's fascination. My whole life, from kindergarten to my retirement from the CIA, when Mom swept into the room, everything stopped and everyone stared. She was good. Mom could make anyone feel like the only person on earth, whether you were an astrophysicist or a ditch digger. Was that still a job—ditch digger?

"So, you have a date now! Way to go, Judith!" Kelly grinned.

"December 15." Mom nodded. "We should use your church too, Kelly. It's probably the closest thing to religion Merry has here."

Ugh. Kelly's church had mixed memories for me. We'd had a lock-in for our troop there once, which ended with Philby being dyed pink and a dead body in the kitchen.

"I'm amazed," Kelly said as she absently disengaged Finn from chewing on what looked to be a very expensive necklace worn by Mom (who didn't seem to care at all). "That you remember to call your daughter Merry, when you've called her Finn her whole life."

"There's only one Finn now," Mom baby-talked to my namesake, who cooed and gave her a crooked grin. "Besides, Merry suits her."

Oh, she was good.

Mom held Baby Finn as I gave her the tour of my little ranch-style house. If she had criticisms over my horribly disfigured coffee table (a curse upon IKEA), the mattress riddled with bullet holes in the guest room, the complete lack of décor, the junk food-filled fridge, and my boring bathroom and bedroom, she said nothing. The woman could be the best diplomat ever in the scariest place on earth. And, for your information, that is Luxemburg. Never go there.

Kelly and the baby left right around noon.

"Let's go eat," Mom said. "It's lunchtime, and I've been dying for a burger from Oleo's."

I agreed and grabbed my keys. "We should probably get you a rental car too."

Even though Mom would be staying just two days, she'd need her own vehicle to get around so she wasn't trapped when I wasn't home.

Oleo's, the bar with the best burgers in Iowa, was packed, but we found a nice quiet booth in the back. After ordering, Mom pulled a leather-bound portfolio from her bag and took the cap off a Mont Blanc pen.

"We need to start a list."

I grimaced. "This is when this stuff gets overwhelming."

"It doesn't have to be. We already have a date and possible church. Tomorrow I'll see if they have December 15 available, and I'll start to check out reception sites. We've gotten a lot done already."

"Then what do we need a list for?"

The waitress handed me a glass of tea and gave Mom a cup of coffee.

"Organization," Mom said. "Let's start with something basic. What's your favorite color?"

"Green. Oh, and I also like white." That was easy. Hopefully all the questions would be like this.

"Perfect. Now we know what your colors will be. We can do white flowers, like roses, iris, or peace lilies. Your bridesmaids can wear green, which will fit in nicely with the holidays, and the décor for the reception hall will be green and white."

Oh, hey. Those were Girl Scout colors. Did I have that on the brain, or did I really like green and white? They seemed like boring colors, but considering that I also liked black and gray (and I was too lazy to really give it any thought), I decided to stick with green and white.

"You're joking," I snorted. "It can't be that easy."

The waitress arrived and took our orders. Both of us got the jumbo burger baskets, because *duh*. I never understood people who went to a burger joint and got salads. It seemed un-American. It was certainly un-Iowan.

"It is that easy. Tonight we can look through those magazines and get an idea of what the bridesmaids and flower girl will wear."

"Well, that sounds okay…"

I wasn't sure who my bridesmaids would even be. Obviously Kelly would be maid of honor. And I knew twelve little girls who would jump at the chance. Granted, I'd have to set rules, such as no weapons or fire-starting, and we'd probably have to have s'mores at the reception —but that might work.

And then there was my old friend, Maria Gomez. I'd have loved to invite her…of course I had no idea where she was or how to get hold of her. My CIA colleague had gone rogue the previous month, over something she called "scruples."

The waitress dropped off our food, and Mom swooned. I guess it'd been a long time since she'd eaten like this. We ate in silence, enjoying the grease and the red meat. It was definitely an Iowa thing. There weren't many dinners in my youth that didn't involve a steak or pot roast or meatloaf. Well, occasionally we had chicken or pork chops just to shake things up a bit, but meat was always on the menu.

The crowd was thinning out because lunchtime was over. I knew we couldn't eat too late because Rex was taking us to dinner. Not that I ever had a problem eating. Fortunately I had a high metabolism. Which was good because a few weeks ago I'd eaten two cans of SpaghettiOs over the sink for dinner.

After picking up the rental car and heading home, my mother and I spent the rest of the afternoon looking through the wedding magazines.

Did you know there are three million types of dresses? And they are expensive? And you only wear them once? Mom said something about handing it down to my daughter, but I broke out in heart palpations and she stopped pressing the issue.

We dog-eared the pages we liked and worked our way through the lot before it was time to get ready for dinner.

"Ladies"—Rex smiled—"you look wonderful." The man knocked this time, out of respect for my mother. He was so handsome in a black suit and blue tie. Goosebumps popped up all over me in all the right places.

"So do you!" I stepped forward and kissed him properly this time.

My mother beamed. I hadn't really had much time to think about what she and Dad thought of my getting married. I guess they approved, because they didn't ask me to reconsider.

They had met Rex during my troop's trip to DC and told me every chance they got that I was so lucky to have found him. I wasn't sure that was a compliment, because shouldn't he be lucky to have me? After all that's happened over the last two years, maybe they were right. I was kind of a ticking time bomb of disaster—even when it wasn't my fault.

Rex drove to Des Moines, and I insisted Mom sit up front with him. They chatted as if they'd known each other forever. My heart felt like it was about to burst with pride. What was my problem? Marrying Rex would be wonderful, and I had no doubt we'd be happy. So why was I so filled with dread?

Just outside of Des Moines, we stopped at a Greek restaurant called Syma's. Greek columns peppered the stucco walls outside.

"This is new! How did you find out about this place?" I whispered as Rex helped me out of the car.

"Officer Dooley told me. He's eaten here three times in the last week."

"Kevin drives all the way here to eat? I thought he just ate at the Stop-N-Go on 7th Street," I said, but Rex was already around the car to help Mom out.

Rex opened the door to the restaurant too and held our chairs while we sat down. Such a gentleman. My mother was impressed, and I was too. Now if only he'd talk to me about his family, I might be a little less doubtful.

The interior of Syma's was dazzling white with a frieze of the Aegean Ocean on the wall and a fresco of the Gods on Mt.

Olympus on the ceiling. I thought Zeus looked a bit like Rex. In fact, he looked a *lot* like Rex.

I shook my head to clear it because I was clearly superimposing my handsome fiancé's face onto a Greek God's body.

My thoughts returned to the present as the fragrance of fish and lamb mingled with the scent of freshly baked bread. My stomach rumbled, and my mouth watered. Riley and I had been stationed very briefly in Greece when we were chasing Carlos the Armadillo. Unfortunately, the Colombian drug lord had only stayed a week. I was so smitten with the food, I could've killed him. Oh wait, I did…later. Too bad it was with my old car. But that story is for another time.

A waiter brought us a bottle of champagne. I didn't remember us ordering that.

"I called ahead," Rex explained.

The waiter popped the cork and poured three glasses before bowing and vanishing.

"How thoughtful!" Mom reached for her glass and held it up. "Okay. You can marry my daughter."

We clinked glasses and drank. As the bubbles tickled my throat, I found myself relaxing.

"Too bad Dad couldn't come," I said as I picked up the menu.

"He's very busy these days. There's a major bill going through the Senate right now, and he's had so many meetings…" Mom said. "Lately I spend most days alone in the house. This is so nice."

I felt a little pang of sympathy for her.

"But don't feel sorry for me. That's the way a politician's wife lives." Her graceful smile absolved us of pity.

"You should get a hobby or something," I suggested. I was going to suggest cat breeding, but Dad wasn't too fond of the little beasts.

"I've thought about it," Mom answered, "and I do have many friends in DC. I just need to get out more."

My stomach rumbled, reminding me it had been a while since the sinful burger basket at Oleo's. I opened the menu and gazed longingly at the list of appetizers.

Rex smiled warmly. "I'm so happy you're here, Judith. You've already made huge strides in getting Merry to commit to the wedding plans."

I frowned. He kind of made me sound like I was a dog she'd taught to sit, beg, and roll over.

She laughed. "You'll get used to it. I think the whole reason Merry joined the CIA was to avoid long-term commitments."

"Hey!" I protested. "I make long-term commitments! I have pets, a mortgage, and a Girl Scout troop." All fine, long-term commitments. Sure, I didn't have a calendar or even a watch, but I was in this for the long haul.

"But honestly," Mom smoothly covered, "I've never seen her so happy as she is when she's around you."

Rex actually blushed. It was so adorable that I leaned over and kissed him. We weren't normally big on public displays of affection. But here I was, kissing my fiancé in public. It made me realize my mother was right. Rex made me happy.

"Have you thought about groomsmen?" Mom asked.

Rex shrugged, "Not really. I was thinking of a simple ceremony."

"Surely you have friends or family…" she started.

I came to his rescue. "How about we just have a best man and maid of honor? I'll talk to Kelly."

Rex bit his lip. I'd never seen him do that before. Whom would he choose for his best man? I'd never really met any friends of his. As long as he didn't pick Kevin Dooley. I pictured me walking up the aisle while Kevin munched on pork rinds…

And then it hit me—the family he didn't acknowledge. I had an idea. Tomorrow Mom and I would go to visit his sisters in the taxidermy shop. She'd win Ronni the angry twin over, and I could start getting to know them.

"There's plenty of time for that," Mom soothed as the waiter returned to take our orders.

Watching Rex as he ordered, I realized that talking about Rex's family was off-limits. That seemed like a problem. A committed couple should be able to talk about anything, right?

"So," Rex said. "December 15th is the date, and we're using the Lutheran Church. Where should we have the reception?"

"What about the old Peters lumber mill?" my mother asked. "It's right there on Main Street, and when I drove by it today, and they have a sign up saying it's a reception hall now."

Rex choked on his glass of champagne. Of course, he wouldn't want it there. The building was next door to his sisters'. He must've known I'd use any excuse to drop by, like borrowing tape or severed animal heads. My troop would like that.

"That's a great idea!" I nudged Mom. "Who owns it now?"

Mom shrugged. "It might be owned by whoever lives in the old Peters place. I see it's been turned into a taxidermy shop. Why don't we run by in the morning and ask?"

Rex coughed again. "The Radisson would be nice."

"That's too far," Mom said. "The lumber mill is right on Main, a few blocks from the church." She turned to him. "Don't worry, Rex. We can take care of this one, right, Merry?"

I grinned wickedly. "That's a great idea, Mom."

The food arrived before Rex could speak up, and we dug in. I loved Greek food. Especially stuffed grape leaves. I had the lamb while Mom and Rex ate seafood. And during the whole course, I realized that the next day, Randi and Ronni were going to find out they'd be getting a new sister. Of course, they'd love me. I'm fun!

I'd have to get Rex to move on introducing the rest of his family. They should meet my mother before the ceremony. And whatever had driven his family apart, Judith Czrygy should be able to patch it up easily.

My fiancé and mother chatted amiably through the rest of the dinner. It was so good to see them together, I felt a pang of homesickness…which was weird because technically, I *was* home. Dad would need to come visit. Maybe we could go to dinner with the Fergusons. Providing the sisters didn't bring dead animals with them, they'd probably hit it off.

Finally, I joined into the conversation as we talked about the guest bedroom furniture.

"What happened in there, Merry? You kind of rushed me through, but I noticed the holes in the bed and closet door."

Rex told Mom about how I'd shot up the bed and closet. She laughed, which was good because it meant she wasn't worried about me having a gun.

"I'm thinking of buying new furniture," I interrupted.

The two of them stared at me.

Uh-oh. What had I done? "What?"

"I just don't know why you'd want to do that since in less than a year, you'll be moving in with me," Rex said.

Oh man. That was one thing I hadn't considered. One of us would have to sell our house. I loved my house. It was my first. And yes, there'd been some murders at the place, but I couldn't imagine not living there forever. As a spy, I'd moved around so much that I didn't really belong anywhere. Owning a house was a huge deal for me.

My mother spoke up. "Of course. Rex's house is larger. In fact, I'd love a tour sometime."

"I hadn't really thought about selling the house…" I muttered.

"It doesn't make sense to have two houses, Merry," Rex said softly as he placed his hand over mine.

Maybe we could turn it into a meeting house for my troop? The idea had merit. I could put bunk beds in the bedrooms and a large table and chairs in the living room. Philby and Martini would always be permitted of course.

I snapped out of it. "I'm sure you're right. It's just the first time I've thought about it."

Mom listened as Rex began to describe the house to her. My mood, however, remained cloudy. I really didn't want to sell the house. But keeping it and using it for other stuff might be okay.

After an hour, the waiter appeared, and Rex asked for the bill.

"But sir, your bill has been taken care of. No charge for you or your charming dinner companions."

Rex seemed confused. "I think there's been some kind of mistake…"

The waiter shook his head furiously. "No sir. Thank you for your business."

He disappeared before we could ask him anything else. Once again, my eyes drifted to the Rex as Zeus painting on the ceiling.

"Do you know the owners?" Mom asked.

My fiancé shook his head and frowned. "I've never been here before. I have no idea why they'd pay for my dinner."

As we drove home, my fiancé and mother had moved on to talking about the cats, but I was staring out the window, into the night, thinking about how he avoided mentioning the twins. The discussion, or lack thereof, of Rex's family and my house seemed like big obstacles to overcome.

At least tomorrow I'd out myself to his sisters. And they'd probably love me, and all the problems would melt away.

Right?

CHAPTER SEVEN

───────

Kelly called first thing the next morning. "I scheduled the meeting with the vulture at the zoo for this afternoon right after school."

"Today?" was all I could manage. Once again, I hadn't slept much. All I could think about was losing my house.

"It was the only time they could do it. I guess the bird has a busy schedule."

I didn't respond.

"Are you okay? Did you get any sleep last night?" my best friend asked.

"I think you need to put me into a medically induced coma," I said at last.

"I can't do that, and you know it."

"How about Dr. Body? She could do it, right?" I asked, referring to our local coroner, Soo Jin Body.

"Nobody can do it. You just have to relax," Kelly said.

"I'm not sure that's possible." I didn't want to tell her my feelings on the wedding. "I've become obsessed with watching the neighbors. Last night was the first time I didn't stare at them through the garage window."

"The Fontanas?" Kelly asked.

"You know them too?"

I could swear I heard her eyes roll. "Of course. They handle my insurance."

There was a silence as I processed this. Slowly.

"Merry, you have to do something about this," she warned. "You could fall asleep while driving or worse. The hospital is doing a sleep study. Why don't I sign you up?"

"M'okay," I mumbled as the room started to blur.

"In the meantime, I'll pick you up for the zoo at 3:30, okay?"

I didn't answer.

"Merry?" My mother's worried face loomed over me, and I sat up. "Maybe we shouldn't go out this morning." How did she get in? Did I give her a key? I couldn't remember.

The thought made me jump to my feet. "Oh no! You have to meet them!"

Mom frowned. "Meet them? Meet who?"

"I never told you about Rex's family, did I?"

I filled her in on Randi and Ronni, how they were polar opposites who looked alike. How they took dead animals and gave them human clothing. Mom listened carefully as she made breakfast. I spotted the grocery bags on the counter and realized she'd been to the store before coming over.

"They don't know who you are? And they haven't contacted their brother since they moved here?" Mom frowned. "How very odd."

At last! Sympathy for the fact that Rex had kept his family from me.

"Still, every family has its quirks," she said as she scooped out the eggs and bacon and plopped them expertly on two plates.

I picked up a slice of bacon and began munching. "Not ours. We're pretty normal, right?" Well, normal for a senator and his wife from Iowa who have a spy for a kid, that is.

My mother laughed. "Not really. I have an Aunt June I never told you about. And then there's your father's cousin Toad."

That got my interest. "Dad has a cousin named Toad?"

"Yup. He died a while back. Was hit by a car. Well, technically, he jumped in front of the car."

"Jumped...like a toad?"

Mom nodded. "It was quite fitting, actually. He always wore green and sometimes ate flies."

"How did I not know I had a cousin named Toad?"

"No one really liked him. Now Toad's brother Sal..."

"That's a normal name! How did his brother get saddled with—"

"…amander, he's okay. He's a biologist in Scotland."

I stared at my mother as she started washing up.

"Are we inviting Salamander to my wedding?" Was I going to have to write *Salamander Czrygy* on an actual invitation?

My mother shrugged. "We haven't really kept in touch."

"And Aunt June?"

"When you were little, your grandmother, about once a month, would call and tell us something about Aunt June. I'd never heard of her. Still haven't seen so much as a photo. But my mother insisted she was real."

"Well, I don't know about that, but Ronni and Randi are very real."

"What's wrong?"

"It bothers me that Rex hasn't told his family about me. It's like he's embarrassed about me."

"I doubt that. He probably is embarrassed about them."

"Maybe…but why keep them a secret? They've been here a month, and he only mentioned it because I pressed him."

"Let's go see them." Mom folded the dishtowel and placed it on the counter. "It's time they get to know their fabulous future sister-in-law."

The gunshot noise went off the minute we pushed through the door. I'd forgotten to tell Mom. She acted as though nothing unusual had happened. I guessed that years of being a senator's wife had trained her not to react to the outrageous.

I, on the other hand, flinched. Couldn't help it. Years of being a spy trained me that gunshots were bad things.

"Wow," Mom murmured under her breath. "I think you understated the situation a bit."

We were surrounded by dead animals, two or three times more than when I'd first come in there. And all arranged into bizarre scenarios. There were two wolves in three-piece suits, playing shuffleboard. A bobcat was wearing a leotard and ballet slippers and was in position number two. Four chickens were involved in a strange runway fashion shoot, and a badger was playing a French horn.

"This is new," I said.

"Hello!" Randi came around the corner, wiping her hands on her apron. "Sorry about the delay. I'm working on a custom order in back and didn't hear the bell."

She shook our hands and smiled. I really liked her. Maybe Ronni wasn't around and we could have a nice conversation.

"Randi!" her twin growled as she came around the corner. She was holding a turkey on her left hand as if it was a puppet. And by that, I mean her hand was *inside* the turkey. "Where's the glue?" It was a question that sounded more like an angry curse.

"In the workshop on the green stool," Randi answered without looking at her sister.

"Who are you?" Ronni scowled at my mother and me.

"What a lovely shop you have!" Mom purred. "I'm Judith, and this is my daughter, Merry."

Randi shook our hands warmly as Ronni simmered in place. Randi introduced her sister and herself. And the four of us just stood there, looking at each other, surrounded by animals that were looking at us.

I wondered how Mom was going to smooth this over.

"A taxidermy business is just what this town needs!" Mom clapped her hands together. "I don't know why we never had one before!"

I tried to picture the musical badger in my parents' house in DC. It was impossible. And I was so buying it for them for Christmas.

"That's so sweet!" Randi blushed. "No one else has said that since we've moved in."

"Have you had a lot of business?" I asked.

"We do mostly online sales," Ronni snapped. "Why are you here? Didn't the crow work out? Typical. You're just a looky-loo. Came here to spy and bought something to cover. Then you return it later. I knew it!"

"No, I love the crow." I held my hands up, ignoring the fact that she was right about the spy part. You never knew when you'd be in a defensive situation. And this seemed to be turning into one. "In fact, I gave it to my fiancé. He loves it."

I'd planned to tell these two about Rex and me. I just thought I'd be able to ease into it after some small talk and a slight lie.

"Whatever," Ronni snapped.

"Please excuse my sister," Randi apologized. "She's okay. Just a little defensive about our work."

"No problem." My mother smiled. "I admire people who are passionate about what they do."

The four of us stood there in silence, staring at each other. I had my eye more on Ronni. If she attacked, I'd take her down, future family or no future family.

"Were you looking for something else?" Randi radiated warmth. Maybe I could spend holidays with her and not her surly sister. But Rex said they'd never been apart, so that probably wouldn't work out.

"Actually…" I bit my lip. What if they didn't like me? Would that impact my engagement? Would I have to fill my house with shuffleboard-playing wolves to smooth this over?

"I wanted to introduce myself last time. I was just distracted by"—I looked into the eyes of a moose who was shaving a billy goat's beard—"all this cool stuff."

The women looked at me expectantly. My heart flip-flopped in my rib cage.

"I'm Merry Wrath. And I'm…"

The shotgun sound went off.

"My fiancé," Rex said as he stood in the doorway.

How did he know what I was going to say? I looked around and saw the windows were open. That, and the fact Mom and I had told him we were coming here.

Rex made no move toward his sisters. He folded his arms over his chest as if waiting for a typhoon to settle in.

"Rexley!" Randi squealed and hurled her tiny self into his arms.

Rexley? I wondered if it was spelled Rexli. That was *not* going on the wedding program.

My fiancé hesitated but finally hugged his sister back, looking a little confused, as if he'd been expecting a different reaction.

Randi extricated herself and flew into my arms. I hugged her, not really knowing how else to respond. I maintained a defensive stance, however, in case she had hidden taxidermy knives.

"I can't believe it!" Randi looked at me, eyes shining. "I'm so happy for you both!"

This didn't seem like an awkward reunion between estranged siblings.

"Isn't that wonderful, Ronni?" Randi returned to her sister's side.

"You broke my armadillo!" Ronni scowled at her brother.

He rolled his eyes. "When I was four! I can't believe you're still holding a grudge about that."

"You broke her armadillo?" I asked slowly. "How do you break an armadillo?"

"Stay out of it!" Ronni screamed before disappearing into the back of the shop.

Randi hugged my mother. "So happy to meet you both!" She slid her arm through Rexli's. "It's been so long! Too long. Now, let me run back into the kitchen and make a pot of tea. Don't you go anywhere!"

She vanished.

"See?" Mom grinned. "That wasn't too bad, now was it?"

"What are you doing here?" I asked Rex. "And thank you for coming. I think Ronni was about to kill and stuff me."

My fiancé didn't even look around at the bizarre dioramas. "I couldn't let you do this on your own. This is my family. My responsibility." He kissed me on the forehead. "And it went way better than I thought it would."

"It did?"

"Last time I saw Ronni, she sucker-punched me with a beaver."

I would've paid good money to see that. And I made a mental note to write *No dead animals allowed* on our wedding invitations.

"Randi seemed happy about our engagement."

He stared off into the distance beyond the door. "She did, didn't she? Huh."

"You're surprised?" I asked.

Mom wandered off to check out a poker game played by some shifty-looking guinea pigs.

Randi's voice called out from the other room, "Do you like sugar in your tea?"

"No thanks," Rex called back, then whispered to me, "maybe you should let me drink first."

My eyes went wide. "Poison?"

"I don't think she'd go that far. But diuretics are a definite possibility."

"Why would she do that?" I asked as Rex's sister burst through the doorway with a tray.

We followed her into another room, where vultures surrounded a tea table with an embroidered linen tablecloth. I sat down, avoiding looking up. At least she didn't have a king vulture. If I brought the girls here and the twins had something that looked like Mr. Fancy Pants, they wouldn't like it.

"Randi," Rex started.

She silenced him. "Now Rexley, I know we left on bad terms, but I'm so happy for this little reunion and your wonderful news!"

"Yes." Rex cautiously sampled a scone. "I can see that. The question is, why?"

His statement seemed to make his sister sad.

"You two...three..." I said, "can work that out later." Preferably when I wasn't around.

"I like her." Randi elbowed her brother as she sipped her tea. "Has she met Mom and Dad?"

I turned to look at Rex.

"We decided to tell you and Ronni first." Rex winked at me.

We were headed into strange territory now. I had no idea what his parents were like. They couldn't be any stranger than the twins, could they?

I dove in. "But we'd love to tell them as soon as possible."

Randi set down her tea and gave her brother a look I couldn't decipher.

"You should. You can't keep this from them, and you can't hold what they did against them."

"What did they do?"

"After all, arranged marriages aren't all that uncommon." She handed me a cookie.

"Arranged marriages?" I gasped. "You're joking." Had I missed something in his background? I thought of the cultures that participated in arranged marriages, but Rex wasn't Indian or medieval royalty.

A muscle twitched in my fiancé's jawline.

"How interesting!" Mom cooed. "Tell us about it."

Rex didn't look like he wanted to tell us about it.

His sister waved us off. "It was a very long time ago. Mom and Dad have some, well, unusual beliefs." She lowered her voice and looked around carefully. "We are Congregationalists, you know." Randi sat back and smiled. "Besides, they would never have held you to it."

"Until I broke it off in middle school." Rex was very quiet. I knew that look as the calm before the storm.

In all honesty, I'd never seen Rex angry. He had a level head that always prevailed no matter what I'd gotten up to.

"Who were you supposed to marry?" I asked.

Rex refused to say anything. I had a bad feeling about this.

"You don't know her, I'm sure." Randi said. "It was a long time ago. And it wasn't legally binding."

"She thought so." Rex grimaced.

"Who?" I repeated.

"Well sure, the poor girl was brokenhearted. She'd loved you since you were five years old. You had to expect a few tears."

"Tears?" Rex stared incredulously. "She and her family threatened to sue me over something that wasn't even legal. Mom and Dad stopped speaking to me. A few tears?"

I set my teacup down. "Your arranged bride was going to sue you?"

"Well, they didn't, did they?" Randi patted his hand. "Besides, it was a long time ago."

Rex said nothing.

"She's probably forgotten all about it and moved on, right?" Randi asked.

Rex still said nothing.

I had a *very* bad feeling about this.

"Let's talk about something else," Mom said, ever the diplomat.

"I'm sure I'm right about Julie…" Randi said.

"Julie?" I squeaked.

Rex sighed heavily. Clearly, he'd hoped this was going to go in a different direction. "Julie is short for Juliette."

CHAPTER EIGHT

———

"Juliette Dowd?" I screamed as we walked to our cars. "You were promised to that psycho? No wonder she hates me!"

"Who's Juliette?" Mom seemed confused and alarmed.

"A redheaded demon who has tried to make my life hell." I was shaking with rage. "Of all the people for you to have been betrothed to—Juliette Dowd!"

Rex put his arm around me, but I pulled away. He'd kept too many secrets from me lately, and I wasn't happy.

"Anything else I don't know about you?" I stormed. "Any children? A career as a stripper? Have *you* murdered anyone?"

It shocked me just how much about my fiancé I didn't know. From the first dead body he investigated attached to me, I've been upfront with him. There's no way I thought he had secrets from me. And Juliette Dowd? Really?

"Merry"—Rex held his hands up—"I didn't mean to keep you in the dark. In spite of what she thought, we were never a couple."

"And yet, here we are," I grumbled. Turning to the shop, I thought I saw a curtain flicker. His sisters were watching.

"This is why I didn't tell you." He looked at the window. "My family is toxic. They love to cause trouble."

"How can you say that? Randi was great! She was so nice about everything! She made us tea!"

He gave me a look. "And yet, she still made sure the first thing she said was about this whole arranged marriage thing."

I opened my mouth and then closed it. He was right. That's exactly what she did.

"Your family is something else," I said finally. "And I have too much going on to deal with it right now. Head back to work. I've got a meeting with a king vulture."

He looked stunned. But he nodded and did what I asked. He gave me one last glance before he drove away.

Blood was roaring in my ears as Mom drove back to my house. Rex lied by not telling me the truth. That really bothered me. Way more than I'd have thought. He knew everything about me, from my former job to my one-time fling with Riley.

And I knew next to nothing about him. Was this a deal breaker? Should I call the wedding off? What else didn't I know? Since he didn't have any groomsmen in mind, was his best man going to be a dead polar bear on wheels?

Kelly was waiting for me when we got back. "It's 3:30," my best friend said. "Let's go!"

Mom decided to stay and make some calls to caterers. She insisted I go to the meeting. Kelly started pulling out of the driveway before I even had the door shut.

We drove in the direction of the zoo. Most people would find it odd that a small town would have a zoo. About seventy-five years ago, a prominent doctor in town decided that we needed our own hospital. At the grand opening he announced that we also needed a zoo because, as he said, "You can't have one without the other."

No one knew what that meant then, but he spent a small fortune on the facility, and when he died, he endowed both the hospital and the zoo with fifty million dollars. Each. This confused people because no one knew he'd had that kind of money. Dr. Aken had spent his whole life in Who's There, driven a beat-up car several decades out of date, and lived in a tiny ranch house.

There had been rumors that the money had been ill-gotten, but nobody ever found a link. And the hospital and zoo fought to keep it quiet.

So, we have a state-of-the art hospital and an impressive, if small, zoo. We even had an elephant. Obladi Zoo was just outside of town. For decades Whovians (people from Who's There) believed the word Obladi meant "shining bear." A few years back, a cultural historian from the University of Iowa was giving a talk at the library on the languages of the Ioway and Ho Chunk tribes. A little kid asked Professor Higgins to confirm the meaning. The professor told the astonished audience that Obladi meant nothing and suggested the late Dr. Aken had been drinking while listening to the Beatles.

Higgins has never been invited back.

We pulled into the parking lot where our girls stood, literally vibrating with excitement over seeing their beloved Mr. Fancy Pants again.

"Good afternoon!" A tall, middle-aged woman joined us. "Are you the Girl Scout troop?"

I grabbed Betty and clapped my hand over her mouth before she could say something rude.

"We are." Kelly smiled. "Girls, this is Dr. Wulf. She's the executive director of the zoo!"

The girls nodded as if they'd always known this.

Dr. Wulf stepped forward. She was wearing a tailored pantsuit on her slim frame. She brushed a strand of silver hair from her face.

"We are very excited to have you visit the king vulture."

Lauren blurted out, "His name is Mr. Fancy Pants."

If she was surprised by this, the director didn't show it. "That's better than what we've been calling him. Let's go with that."

I made a mental note to give a nice donation to the zoo.

We followed Dr. Wulf into the zoo. It hadn't opened yet for the season, so we didn't have to worry about buying tickets. The zoo had changed a lot since I'd been there as a kid. For one thing, it was filled with colorful signs about the exhibits. There were interactive displays and huge flowering trees.

"Hey!" I shouted. "They still have the train! Can we ride the train?"

Dr. Wulf gave Kelly a questioning glance, to which Kelly rolled her eyes.

"I think we can make that happen another day," she said. "The train conductor is out of town."

We were cool.

At last we entered what looked like an educational center. I knew this because there were no animal signs. As we walked through the building, I noticed a huge aquarium taking up a full wall. Then, we walked into some sort of classroom. Standing on a large branch was the king vulture. His eyes were covered with that mask they use on falcons. Why was that, I wondered. He kind of looked like a bird version of Hannibal Lecter.

The girls beat me to the question.

"Why is he blindfolded?" Hannah the First (I also have two Hannahs) asked. The other girls all nodded.

If I hadn't seen Fancy Pants in action back in DC, I would've thought this a fair question. The bird was obsessed with cookies. Especially Girl Scout cookies. I patted my purse and felt the box of shortbread cookies inside. I wasn't sure if I was going to bring it out in the open.

"We've noticed," Dr. Wulf said, "certain inappropriate behaviors of Mr. Fancy Pants. We've had to change his keeper twice because, apparently, when he sees cookies, he tackles people."

"That's so cool!" Inez clapped her hands together. I'd forgotten the girls didn't know this.

"He could be a superhero—fighting bad guys with cookies!" one of the Kaitlyns said.

"But what if he attacked Cookie Monster?" Ava asked.

Dr. Wulf held her hands up. "It's okay, ladies. There are no cookies in here."

I blanched. Bringing the cookies might not have been the best idea. Could he smell them? Did birds smell anything?

Kelly motioned to the girls, who took their seats around a large table.

"Who can tell me where king vultures are from?" the director asked.

Twelve hands went up. She called on Emily.

"Central and South America," the girl said.

"Right!" She handed the child something.

Emily held it up. It was like a baseball card, but with Mr. Fancy Pants on it. I wondered if it had stats. Every girl in the room flung their hands into the air. We weren't leaving here until at least eleven more questions were answered. Preferably by a different girl each time.

"What do they eat?" the doctor asked. She chose Caterina.

"Dead things!" the girl squealed.

"Right!" Dr. Wulf said as she handed out another card. "Carrion is the remains of a dead animal. Lizards, rats, anything."

The girls were rocking back and forth in their seats, waiting for the next question.

"Does anyone know how long they live?" she asked.

Again, twelve hands went up in the air. Kelly walked over and physically pushed Emily's and Caterina's hands down in an attempt to let the other girls have a chance.

"Thirty years in captivity!" Lauren answered when called upon.

"Wow!" Dr. Wulf handed her a card. "You girls have done your homework!"

I didn't doubt it for one minute. My girls were addicted to animals and frequently obsessed about them. At Girl Scout camp they'd spent almost a whole year mourning Cookie the Horse, who the equestrian director said was going to have to go. You'd have thought she'd said "glue factory" from the way the girls keened and wailed. Kelly and I endured many months of memorials for Cookie, only to find out that camp had decided to keep him after all.

I wondered how Mr. Fancy Pants would've felt about Cookie…

"How do they fly?" the director asked.

Betty blurted it out before being called upon. "They glide on air currents!"

This was a serious breach in protocol. And the girls made their displeasure known immediately by shouting. Mr. Fancy Pants cocked his head from one side to the other, and this made Dr. Wulf nervous.

Kelly saved the day with the Girl Scout quiet sign, and the girls immediately clammed up.

"I apologize," I said to Dr. Wulf. "They mean well. They're just very excited to be here."

I turned and gave the girls an icy death stare, which they promptly ignored.

The executive director smiled and handed the rest of the cards out to the rest of the girls. Sometimes, the simplest solutions are the best.

"I'm so glad you girls are excited. My specialty in college was birds. I'm excited that he's here too." She patted Kelly on the arm. "Does anyone have any questions for me?"

Lauren raised her hand. "Do they lay eggs?" The doctor was about to answer when Lauren asked another question. "And do they throw up in their chicks' mouths?"

A round of *ewwwwws* went up around the table, but this didn't stop those very same girls from waiting expectantly for the answer.

The director laughed. "Yes, they lay eggs. And yes, they regurgitate food for the chick until the baby is old enough to eat on its own."

"Why is he bald?" Hannah the second asked.

"That's a great question! It's so the sun can shine on his head, taking all the bad bacteria out of the carrion when he eats."

Only one hand went up this time.

"Would Mr. Fancy Pants," Ava asked, "eat me if I was dead?"

Kelly groaned. I thought it was a fair question.

"Did he eat the two zookeepers with the cookies?" Inez asked.

"Yes," Dr. Wulf answered. "If you were on the jungle floor in South America and you were dead, he'd eat you." She turned to Inez. "And no, he didn't eat the zookeepers. They work with the bears now. It's much safer."

Betty raised her hand. "What would he start with, if he was to eat Ava, if she was dead in South America?"

Kelly opened her mouth, but I shook my head at her. While I had no problem with Ava, I was curious about the question.

Dr. Wulf frowned. "I think he'd start with the eyes."

A huge cheer went up, causing the vulture to bob and weave. He was getting agitated. Would he jump on the girls blindly?

Dr. Wulf brought her finger to her lips to shush the girls, who immediately went quiet. "If you can be calm, I'll take his hood off."

The nodding around the table was so vigorous I was worried the girls' heads were going to pop off. Dr. Wulf walked over to the large bird and lifted off his hood.

If you've never seen a king vulture before, it's a bit startling. With a purple and black head, googly eyes usually going in different directions, a bright orange and yellow neck, and a bright orange wattle dangling over its beak, you'd probably think you'd stepped into something a three-year-old painted.

Mr. Fancy Pants looked around the room, causing a hushed gasp among the girls.

"King vultures," Dr. Wulf said quietly, "have astounding eye sight. They can spot carrion from very high up in the sky."

The bird continued to fix his stare on each and every girl. Sometimes on two girls at once. Sometimes on two girls at opposite ends of the table at once.

"Some scientists believe," the director continued, "that they have a keen sense of smell also. That they use this to find their dinner."

Uh-oh. I clutched my purse a little tighter. And that's when the bird's eyes turned to me.

"But, we don't know if that's true or not. And as long as none of you has any cookies on you, we probably won't."

Yep. His eyes were definitely locked on to mine. For a moment his gaze flickered to my purse, then back up to me. I'd say those scientists were right. The girls noticed he was staring at me.

Mr. Fancy Pants extended his wings once more.

"Fancy Pants"—Dr. Wulf pointed—"has a five-foot wingspan. King vultures are the largest vultures on the planet." She looked at the bird and frowned.

"Merry…" Kelly said quietly. "You didn't bring anything with you, did you?" She'd carefully avoided the word cookies.

"I should probably step out for a moment," I said as I turned to make my way to the door.

The vulture's eyes followed me. He knew!

"Ms. Wrath," Dr. Wulf said. "Don't go. It'll only set him off. Hand me the you-know-what."

Very slowly I reached into my purse and pulled out the blue box. Fancy Pants' eyes grew wide, and he started to bob up and down. I walked toward him, opening the box as I went. I'm not sure if vultures can drool, but it looked like something was happening.

The vulture now made direct eye contact with the box, staring as if he was using the Force to bring it to him. I popped out one of the sleeves of cookies and opened it, laying half of the cookies at his feet before handing the rest to Dr. Wulf and stepping back.

Birds of prey tear into their food with their sharp beaks. And they look cool doing so. Mr. Fancy Pants was no different. Using his beak to break the cookies, he guzzled them down like the naughty kid who's afraid they will be taken from him if he doesn't.

It was impressive. The bird had gone into the sugar-buzz zone, and I could've sworn once or twice his eyes rolled back in his head.

Dr. Wulf watched him carefully, tucking the box and its remaining sleeve into a drawer. She made no move to stop him or chastise me, which was nice. Maybe I could "adopt" the bird—donate a few hundred dollars for his upkeep. I'd noticed a sign on the way in where you could adopt the giraffes, the sloth, the wolves, or the hissing cockroaches.

Why not the king vulture?

The cookie orgy was over as Mr. Fancy Pants scooped up every last crumb. The girls cheered quietly, causing him to look them over again. Then, he turned his gaze once more onto me.

Within a second his wings opened up, and he'd jumped from his roost and was running across the table toward me.

"He still thinks you have cookies!" I heard one of the girls shout.

Dr. Wulf was right behind him, trying to make a grab, but missed. Mr. Fancy Pants stopped mere inches from my face. He leaned in, as if looking into my soul. His eyes went down to my purse then up to me. He did this two more times. I knew what that meant.

Because I have two cats who do the same thing. And I did to this bird what I did to them when they looked at me like that. I shrugged.

The giant raptor stepped back for a second as if he didn't believe me and was sizing me up as a potential snack. I opened my purse and held it out to him. He stuck his head inside and began rooting around for the cookies. When he didn't find them, he stopped, his head still inside the bag.

Finally, he pulled his head out. A pen was in his beak. After giving me a look that I think he thought would chill me to the bone, the vulture took the pen, wandered back across the table, and got back onto his perch.

"Okay, ladies!" Dr. Wulf said brightly. "Let's all get up slowly and file out the door, okay?"

The girls reluctantly did what she asked, and Kelly followed. I was right behind her when I stopped to look back at the bird. He wasn't on his perch.

Instead, he was at the drawer where Dr. Wulf had stashed the cookies. He inserted the pen into the rectangular drawer pull and tugged. The drawer opened, and he snagged the box and went back to his perch.

"It's amazing, isn't it?" Dr. Wulf said. "I think maybe those scientists are right...he can smell the cookies."

A woman dressed in coveralls joined us in the room. Dr. Wulf gave her a nod and whispered a few words to her before ushering me out to where the girls were now ogling the giant aquarium.

"I'm sorry about that," I said. "Really. My mind hasn't been right lately, and I've gotten very little sleep..."

Dr. Wulf waved me off. "It's okay. No one got hurt, and you all signed waivers absolving us of any issues anyway."

We did?

"Would it be possible for me to adopt him?" I asked her. "Donate money every month for his upkeep?"

Dr. Wulf stared at me. "That's a great idea! And very generous!"

I gave her my cell number and email address, and she promised to look into it. We herded the girls into the parking lot and waited for their parents to pick them up.

"That went well, I think," I said to Kelly.

She sighed. "I can't believe you brought those cookies. What were you thinking?"

I shrugged but didn't answer. Mostly because I wasn't sure myself. The parents arrived all at once, and after getting the right girls to the right cars—something more difficult with the Kaitlyns—we headed to Kelly's van. That's when I noticed a vehicle slowly driving by.

Kelly squinted. "Do you think that woman looks like Rex?"

Ronni was alone, driving a nondescript van and staring at the zoo. Against my own better judgment, I waved her down. She responded by scowling and racing off.

"Do you think she does taxidermy for the zoo?" I asked as I got into Kelly's car. "I haven't heard of an animal dying in years."

"Maybe she's going to knock one off so she can stuff it," Kelly said.

My future sister-in-law was casing the zoo and possibly plotting against the animals there. That was disturbing.

CHAPTER NINE

———

The route back to my house took us by the city park. It was chilly and starting to drizzle, but Pam Fontana was sitting on a park bench. There weren't any kids around. She was just sitting there, on the bench, in the rain.

"Pull over," I demanded.

"Why?" Kelly asked as she pulled her car into a parking spot.

I didn't answer. Something was happening. I just didn't know what it was.

Kelly squinted. "Is that Pam? What's she doing there?"

I nodded. "That's what I was wondering." I told Kelly about my late-night activities of watching the couple.

She looked at me, stunned. "You've completely lost your mind." Kelly reached for the ignition, but I stopped her.

"Something weird is going on there. The body they carried into the house, the sniper rifle and hatchet…it doesn't make sense."

"Do you think you're projecting these suspicions because you miss work?" Kelly asked.

Her words hit me like a brick wall.

"What? No!" At least, I didn't think so.

"Maybe you should see Susan. She's the counselor at the hospital, and she's good."

"I am not seeing a counselor. I'm not crazy."

"Fine. I'll be your counselor." She turned on the car and turned up the heater. "You're getting married. It's a lot to handle. I don't blame you for going nuts."

"You think I'm going nuts?"

She looked at Pam Fontana for a second and then back at me. "Yes. I think you've lost it."

"That's so unfair!" I whined.

"Is it?" Kelly asked. "You can't sleep. You're forgetting things. You're hallucinating…"

"I am *not* hallucinating!" I hissed. "The stuff I've seen is real! Ask Philby!"

She sighed. "And now you're using your cat as a witness."

Pam Fontana checked her watch before scowling at the sky. If she didn't like the weather, why was she out in it?

"Maybe all of this is your subconscious telling you something?" Kelly continued.

"It's not my subconscious telling me something. It's my intuition. And my intuition has been right for many years."

Pam got up from the bench and walked away.

"She forgot something," I mumbled as I fiddled with my seat belt.

Kelly held me in my seat. "See, this is what I'm talking about. You're seeing plots around every corner. Right now, you're hurting yourself. But you're starting to bring other people down with you. The Fontanas are…"

But I wasn't listening. Because a man I'd never seen before walked past the bench and, without stopping or looking, scooped up whatever it was Pam Fontana had left behind.

"It's a brush pass!" I shouted, pointing at the empty park bench.

Ignoring Kelly, I got out of the car and started running through the now driving rain toward the bench. But the man and whatever he'd taken were long gone.

"What are you doing?" Kelly shouted from the car. "Get back in here!"

There wasn't any reason not to since both Pam Fontana and the man were gone. I made it back to the car, soaking wet, and climbed inside.

Kelly was apoplectic. "That's it! You've officially lost your mind! There wasn't anyone there, and you ran off in the rain to check out something you imagined!"

Wow. She was mad.

"I'm taking you home, and then I'm signing you up for the sleep study. It starts tomorrow."

I began to protest, but she silenced me.

"This is non-negotiable, Merry."

We drove in silence to my house. Mom had left a note saying she was out, talking to the church organist. While I took a hot shower, Kelly made me tomato soup and grilled cheese sandwiches and then watched me eat them.

"Your diet isn't helping either," she mumbled to herself. "Seriously, I think you're driving yourself insane on purpose!"

I refused to be baited, mainly because the soup and sandwich were good and I didn't want her to take them away. Philby and Martini waited for the dregs, but I didn't leave any. Kelly fed them and then shooed me down the hall to my bedroom.

"Get in," she said, holding the sheets and comforter.

"I'm not a baby," I grumbled as I got in. "I'm an adult. You can't treat me this way." Although I was already working on a plan to get her to make me soup and grilled cheese sandwiches more often.

"No." Kelly tucked me in. "You're not a baby. You're a lunatic." She drew the curtains and shut out the light. "I'm calling Judith and telling her what's going on. And now you're going to sleep."

I lay there in the darkness. My mind felt like a nest of squirming snakes. I knew what I'd seen in the park. I was a spy for crying out loud! I knew what a brush pass was. Pam was leaving that…whatever it was…for the stranger. He picked it up without looking at it. Total brush pass!

Why else would she sit out in the rain on a chilly day, in an empty park? There simply was no reason for it. I thought hard about the man. He was very nondescript with dark hair, wearing a raincoat and fedora. I didn't get a look at his face.

The puzzle pieces all clicked into place. I now understood what was going on. The Fontanas were illegals. Not the kind who cross the border from Mexico. *Illegals* was a spy term I knew well.

Mark and Pam Fontana were foreign spies.

Illegals are deep-undercover spies, pretending to be Americans. Sometimes, they spend decades dormant, acting only when needed. It's a long game they play.

Many times they act as a couple. Put together in their home country as total strangers, they spend a lot of time learning how to speak, think, and act American. Some of them even have children when they're here, in order to add to their cover. And in those cases, the agents even fell in love with one another. It was rare, but not unheard of.

Canada! Mark said they'd moved to Minnesota from Canada to attend college. It had to be a dead double. That's when spies find the birth certificate of an infant who died so they can become that person. It helped to get passports, driver licenses— all of the things they'd need to set up here.

My heart was pounding. I'd figured it out. There *was* something wrong with the Fontanas. Rex and Kelly couldn't see it because they weren't trained to do so. I saw it because I was.

The question was, why here? Usually illegals go where there's valuable intel—New York City, Washington DC, places like that. They might live in New Jersey or Maryland or Virginia, but there they have access to politicians. People they can turn.

So why come to this town in the middle of Iowa? Des Moines was thirty minutes away, but it held no charms for espionage. If they were just moving around to establish their bona fides, I'd understand. But Pam just gave someone something. She wouldn't risk blowing her cover unless it was important intel.

And who were they working for? The Russians came to mind. It could be the Chinese, but they'd use their own people. These two didn't look Chinese. They looked like pasty Midwesterners.

I'd figured it out! I wasn't crazy or hallucinating. I was smart. I couldn't wait to rub that in Rex's and Kelly's faces.

But then, they probably wouldn't believe me. They'd think I'd gone completely bonkers if I started screaming about international espionage. Which meant before I could tell them, I'd need more proof. I'd have to break in and search the Fontanas' house. Then I'd have the evidence I needed. Then everyone would know I was right. There was no way I could do it tonight. The Fontanas have proven over and over that they're active in the wee hours.

Tomorrow. After they left for work, I'd head over. That would be the plan.

This, in addition to my insomnia, was killing me. A little rest would go a long way tomorrow. I took a couple of pills and closed my eyes.

I woke up at six in the morning, after four hours of sleep. And even though I know that's not enough, I felt better than I had in a long time. I even made eggs and toast for breakfast, shunning the Lucky Charms.

Mom called.

"Hey Mom, what's up?"

"I'm so sorry, kiddo. I have to head back to DC. Your dad has the flu."

Uh-oh. Taking my mother to the airport would wreck my plan.

"Don't worry about taking me to the airport. I've arranged to drop the rental car there. I really am sorry, Merry. But you know how your dad is when he doesn't feel well."

I smiled. "One of the most powerful men in the USA becomes the most helpless baby."

My mother laughed. "That's right. Now don't worry. I'll keep working on the arrangements."

My shoulders rose up as if a heavy weight had held them down. "Thanks, Mom! Have a safe trip back."

This was great news. Mom could handle the details of the wedding from home. I could continue investigating the Fontanas. Maybe this was what I needed—someone to handle the planning for me.

While I waited, I got dressed. What does one wear to break into a neighbor's house? I could go with my usual black shirt, pants, and boots, but that might attract too much notice if someone saw me, and how would I explain it if the Fontanas came back early?

I always dress like this and thought I'd just pop over...All my other clothes are in the laundry and I needed to borrow detergent...I was painting my bedroom black and thought I could borrow a brush...

I went with a college sweatshirt, jeans, and moccasins. Now I just needed an excuse if I was busted. Got it! I could say that Philby got out and I'd seen her go into their yard. As for why I'd be looking for the cat in their locked house—I'd just have to make something up.

All I needed to do was wait. I sat in the living room watching TV until I saw the car with both neighbors in it back out of the driveway and head down the street. Do you know how much crap they have on television in the mornings? Since when did every single station start a morning show? It's creepy to have complete strangers tell you how they hope you have a great day. They didn't know me. I made a mental note to write in and complain to the local stations in Des Moines. Surely other people were sick of this too.

As much as I hated it, waiting was important. Too many spies have been caught by going into a situation too soon. People forgot things all the time when they left for work. And they were more likely to go back and get it before getting to work. It was better to take the extra time to make sure they were gone for good.

My guess was that these two would put in at least four to six hours of work in their business. If they were home all of the time, folks would get suspicious. Running a strong cover was the key to success as an undercover agent.

One of my first missions had been to track and report on a suspected pair of illegals in Connecticut. Normally the FBI handled that kind of thing, but it had been a special circumstance where the CIA was able to add their own person to the team.

Anyway, Marie and Jessie North had been as careful as they could be. Dormant for years with a couple of young kids, they'd done their jobs very well. It had been the CIA that alerted the Feds to the illegals. Which was part of the reason I'd been assigned.

Both of the Norths had worked at a community college, teaching economics (which, if you ask me, was a dead giveaway). And both were Russian spies. And they'd been in place for ten years before we'd started working on them. I didn't play a huge part in bringing them down because I was just fresh off the Farm—the training compound for the CIA.

It had been a tough assignment. Those two had done such a great job with their cover, it had taken some serious convincing to get the FBI to check them out. My job had been to follow them when they were at work. I'd enrolled in the college as a student and had even taken a class from Marie.

We'd had an entire team on deck. Someone else had followed them the rest of the time. And I didn't have access to that intel. But I'd been the one who'd confirmed they were spies. You never know how you'll get good hard evidence. Sometimes it's strange bank deposits, sometimes you get caught in a brush pass, sometimes your co-workers turn you in. In the case of the Norths, however, it had been a raccoon that brought them down.

As good as they'd been, it had been kind of a noob move to throw microfilm out in the trash. The Norths later blamed it on their eight-year-old son who was a little too ambitious with his chores. But the fact of the matter was that a raccoon had gotten into the trash. A savvy agent had spotted the animal and chased it down, retrieving the evidence. It's the only case in the US that I'm aware of where a wild animal toppled a pair of spies. Outside the US it happens all the time. Usually, it's a chicken. I have no idea why.

These days the Norths are serving time in a maximum-security prison. I felt sorry for the kids. They thought they were Americans, only to get shipped back to Moscow to live with grandparents they'd never known they had, in a country they'd never been to, with a language they'd never spoken. It hardly seemed fair.

After fifteen minutes with no sign of the neighbors, I knew it was safe. I also knew I'd have to go in through their back door to avoid being sighted…especially by Rex. I stuffed my hair into a stocking cap and did a quick check for curly blonde hairs. The Fontanas had brown hair, and there was no point getting busted because I shed the wrong color in their house.

"Okay," I said to Philby. "I'm going in. You're my lookout."

The cat snapped to attention as I made my way to the garage and out into my backyard.

An alley ran behind our properties. I never used it because I had a driveway. But even though the Fontanas had a driveway, they also had a detached garage—which was why I'd been able to see them the other night. It was a strange mistake on their part. An attached garage would've hidden anything. I guess coming in through the alley, as opposed to the busy street, provided some camouflage. Still, I'd take my garage any day. It would be much easier to sneak in a body with an attached garage.

Not that I've ever done that. Okay. Once. Maybe twice.

The back of my yard had thick foliage that gave me a good hiding place as I slipped through the overgrown hedges. Kelly was always on me to trim them, saying something about property values decreasing just by living on my block—whatever that meant. She was naïve. How was I supposed to sneak around without cover?

The garage had a six-foot-tall wooden fence on either side of it. I could scale it, or I could pick the lock on the gate. The lock on the fence looked like a simple padlock. You might think that was a mistake on their part, but if maintaining a cover was more important, they'd have to use a lock like everyone else. They just ran the risk of someone like me living next door with a narcoleptic cat and an insomnia problem.

I pulled on the latex gloves I'd brought and gingerly turned the lock in my hand. It seemed pretty standard, but you never knew. Then, I checked out the fence. I was pretty sure they wouldn't rig it, what with all the school kids who walked down this alley to and from school. But there were other booby traps they might employ.

Running my hands lightly over the fence, I didn't find any tripwires. Everything looked legit. It was possible I was overreacting to this whole thing. The Fontanas could just be weirdos. It's better to be safe than sorry. I opted for saving time and hoisting myself over the fence.

When I landed on the other side, I froze, waiting to see if anything happened. I'm not being paranoid. Booby traps were a pain in a spy's butt. You never knew what to expect. After thirty seconds with nothing happening, I walked over to the door on the other side of the garage. Hmmm…a double-key deadbolt.

That was surprising. My garage and Rex's just had those pushbutton locks in the middle of the knob. It was rare to find a deadbolt on a simple garage door. My pulse quickened. I was right about these two. I picked the lock and quickly stepped inside the dark building and waited.

My eyes adjusted to the murky interior. It would be smart to keep the lights off. And I did have my cell phone if I needed more illumination. The building was empty. Completely empty with not so much as a can of paint or a hammer in sight. This was tip-off number two.

The neighbors didn't use the garage and parked on the street. It was clever, because it made for a quick getaway if they needed it. Backing out of a garage onto an alley that for twenty minutes a day was filled with school kids would impede their running off. I felt validated.

One question remained—why a complicated deadbolt on an empty garage? Now I faced a dilemma. I could spend half an hour at least in here, looking for secret panels and drawers. An hour if I was carefully avoiding traps. It would take me a lot longer than that in the house. But I'd seen the Fontanas carrying the body from the garage into the house. Which meant the decision was made for me.

Relocking the door, I looked both ways as I worked my way down the sidewalk that connected the garage to the back door of the house. Large hedges made an impenetrable border between this house and the next, and with only my house on the other side—and unless they had cameras I couldn't see—I was safe from discovery.

The back of the house had two windows, covered by drapes, and a small kitchen window, also with closed curtains. That seemed strange too. I didn't know a single house that even had kitchen curtains.

I was getting close. My "yay" meter shot up as I set to work, picking the double deadbolt on the back door. It sprung with no problem. Now I really was in dangerous territory. Any spy worth their salt would have all kinds of booby traps, hidden cameras, etc.

The door opened up into a little entryway, not more than nine-foot square. It was a mud porch for folks to leave dirty boots, shoes, etc. I scanned the ceiling for cameras and, finding none, had to make a decision.

I could go directly down into the basement, or left, into the kitchen. Common sense told me to start in the basement and work my way up. It's a thorough way to sweep the house, and if it took a while and someone came home early, it would be easier to escape from the ground floor than from the basement.

The stairs were narrow, and it was dark. A panel on my right had four light switches. That wasn't good. There should be one for the mudroom and one for the stairs with a third possibility being an outside light over the door. But four? That was just madness.

Which also meant the fourth switch could be anything that could hurt me. I'd have to decide quickly which one would turn on the stair light.

I opted for my cell phone instead. It's best to err on the side of caution. Turning on my flashlight app, I carefully held on to the rail and descended into the basement. Each creak, every groan, stopped me in my tracks. At any moment, things could go south quickly. Finally, I landed firmly on the bottom step.

Holding the cell in front of me, I looked around. This appeared to be a normal basement—just like mine. Well, not exactly like mine because I had things like an EVP disruptor, an array of guns, and even a box of tampons that held a hidden camera. Still, nothing would've proved me right like finding stuff like that here in Mark and Pam's basement.

Instead, I found a worktable with the usual tools. Rolls of old wallpaper and a few paintbrushes. I made quick work of this level. I couldn't do a deep search. My hope was I'd find something obvious to prove to Rex that these two were illegals.

I took the stairs a little faster this time and walked into the doorway of the kitchen. These people were fairly neat and organized. While I hoped I'd find a box of Russian cereal or detailed plans to take over the United States, the only thing out of place was the dishwasher.

I smiled. The appliance door was open and the bottom tray was out, empty except for a dozen large knives, blades pointing to the ceiling. This was an old trick. It looks like they just didn't have time to empty the dishwasher, but in fact it was a lethal trap if they were surprised. You just had to throw your opponent down onto the deadly knives. I noticed a small moat of dish liquid on the floor, surrounding the knifey door. One little slip and I'd be dead or dying at worst, seriously injured at best.

Nice.

But that would hardly be enough proof for Rex. And it certainly wouldn't be enough evidence in a court of law.

My eyes swept the room as I carefully pulled open cupboards and drawers. Everything looked normal. I decided to look through the rest of the house. If I had to make a break for it, at least I'd know the layout.

I stopped short at the living room carpet and again congratulated myself. Most people vacuum starting at the farthest corner of the room. Very, very few people vacuum themselves backwards, out of a room.

The difference is in the patterns the machine makes on the carpet. And the reason spies vacuum out of a room backwards onto linoleum is to look for footprints later. Sure, you could make them, but then you'd vacuum like normal and leave. It wouldn't occur to you to do it the way they had. And that would give you away.

The question was, did I have time to run through the house and then find the vacuum cleaner to hide my tracks? The answer was no. But I did have a way to enter the room surreptitiously. Taking off my shoes, I was able to climb onto an end table and walk onto the couch. From there, I was able to survey the room. And what I found was shocking.

The Fontanas didn't have a television. That seemed seriously un-American.

From my vantage point, I could see my living room, and my cat, Philby, standing in the window, paws on the glass, staring at me. What do you know? She did it! I might be able to turn that cat into a proper spy after all.

What was she doing? She was swerving her head from the street, to me, and back again. And again. And that's when I noticed the car coming up the street.

It was the Fontanas. And I was standing on their couch, in the middle of their living room.

I backtracked carefully, which cost me some time. There was no point in making any mistakes. Instead of putting on my shoes, I scooped them up and dodged the dishwasher. I was just letting myself out when I heard the door open on the other side of the house.

There was no time to run up to the gate. They'd see me. Instead, I ran for the hedge that separated my house from theirs and dove over it headfirst. I landed very ungracefully in a heap and managed to crawl to cover behind some shrubs.

The Fontanas' back door opened, and Mark walked out onto the sidewalk, stopping halfway. He looked in all directions for what seemed like an eternity before going back inside.

He didn't see me, but he *knew*.

CHAPTER TEN

———

"Merry?" said a pair of shoes on the ground in front of me. "What are you doing?"

I popped up. "Hi honey!" I kissed him on the cheek. "I was just looking for Martini. I couldn't find her inside the house, so I thought she might have gotten outside."

Rex looked at me. "And you're wearing latex gloves because...?"

I looked down at my hands. "Oh that. Well, I'm mildly allergic to the leaves on some of the shrubs."

It was as good of an excuse as any. Would he buy it?

Rex pointed at the kitchen window. "She's in there."

Martini saw us and immediately ducked out of sight.

"Why are you here?" I brushed the dirt and leaves from my clothes.

My fiancé pulled me into his arms. It was nice. Very nice. I really did love him. People often underestimated Rex—something that was very useful to him as a detective. Oh sure, they probably wondered what I, a former CIA agent, was doing with a small-town detective. But I didn't see it that way. *I* was outclassed. Besides being a total hottie, Rex was a grown-up. He was completely comfortable anywhere. Nothing fazed him. In contrast, I've always been a bit neurotic. I think most spies are.

It was almost a luxury to be around a man who was completely at home in his own skin. I'd never seen him nervous, anxious, or out of sorts. He didn't lose control. Okay, he got angry with me on occasion, but it was a quiet sort of anger. And usually he was right. I just wasn't going to let him know that.

Riley was so unpredictable. And he flirted with anything without a Y chromosome. Charming and handsome, he was also devious and deceptive. With Rex, I knew where I stood. With Riley, I hadn't a clue.

Besides, Rex gave me that warm, gooey feeling inside. His kisses made me quiver, his smile made me feel like I'd won the lottery, and he made me feel special. We fit together like chocolate and peanut butter, like champagne and caviar, like a frazzled Girl Scout leader and a shot of whiskey.

"Just wanted to see you"—he kissed me quickly—"and remind you that Martini has an appointment at the vet's in an hour."

Awesome! "Which was, of course, why I was so worried that she'd gotten outside." To be honest, I had forgotten the appointment.

Rex kissed me softly on the lips. "I have to get back to work. We had a fire at the old ice cream shop on Main, and I'm helping the investigator."

"Another fire? Like the one last month at the arena?"

"Yes. It's probably a coincidence." Rex took my hand and led me inside. "But at least the Tasty Cream has been empty for years. No one was hurt."

We didn't have many fires in Who's There. Maybe one a decade. It seemed strange to have two in two months, and in the spring.

"Good luck." I hugged him before he went out the front door.

I leaned against the door and sort of deflated. Rex had almost caught me. And when we got married, he would be able to watch my every move. In this case, however, I'd dodged a bullet. He'd bought my story about Martini. In the future, once we were living in the same house, this would be much harder to do.

The idea made it feel like my stomach dropped out of my body and crawled away. It was kind of like a cartoon *boing*. This constant case of nerves whenever I thought of getting married was getting old. I needed to figure out what my problem was. Did I need a therapist? I'd never gone to a shrink before. Well, except for the ones at the CIA who analyzed everything you did to make sure you were mentally stable for the field.

I'd never had a problem with that. But I remember one guy—we'll call him Dan. Dan freaked out the first time he was tied up for a simulation. He started crying and begging for mercy, and they hadn't even pretended to torture him yet.

After a few seconds of that, he declared he was a ferret and made some odd little chittering noises before singing a Weird Al Yankovic song and passing out.

I pulled the cat carrier out of the hall closet, and Martini crawled inside and immediately fell asleep. She was a strange kitten. Always ready to crash at the drop of a hat. And she slept so deeply that a number of times, I'd thought she'd slipped into a coma.

As I dragged the carrier out to my van, I revisited the idea of seeing a therapist. Didn't Kelly recommend one to me? My cell was in my hand, but I could only reach the main button, which I hit, instructing the voice on my phone to call my best friend.

"Merry?" My bestie's voice came on. "I'm at work. What's up?"

"I was thinking about what you said…about me being mental about the wedding."

"You're always mental," Kelly murmured.

"Anyway…" I ignored the jibe. "Maybe it would be a good idea to talk to someone. Like a counselor."

Kelly burst with excitement, which I thought was an unusual reaction. "Yes! That's a great idea! You can see Susan! I'll text you her number!"

For some reason, I questioned her. "Is she any good?"

"What do you mean? Why would I recommend someone who isn't good?" There was a touch of annoyance in her voice.

"Maybe you're not Kelly, but someone impersonating her." It could happen.

"I'm hanging up now."

I didn't really think it was an unreasonable statement as I dialed the number Kelly (or the woman impersonating Kelly) texted me and was put through to this Susan immediately.

"Ms. Wrath! Mrs. Albers just told me you'd be calling," a woman with a pleasant and soothing voice said.

This Kelly impersonator works fast.

We made an appointment for forty-five minutes from then. Hopefully, the vet appointment wouldn't take long. Five minutes later, we arrived. Maple Wood Vet Clinic was in a small building on the outskirts of town. Rex had been taking the cats in for their appointments when needed. He'd said they had new staff and a new doctor. I was a little nervous about that.

Huh. I didn't seem to have a problem when Rex ran errands for me. I shouldn't have any problems thinking about our future. What was wrong with me?

Martini slept soundly in the carrier as I walked into the clinic. It took a lot to wake that kitten up. Philby usually growled and hissed. She didn't like going to the vet. We'd had some issues in the past with another clinic—now closed. Moving to a different place did nothing to change Philby's prejudice against doctors.

"Ms. Wrath?" A short, perky young woman in a lab coat stood in front of me.

"Yes," I said. "I'm here with Martini." Maybe it was the lack of sleep or the adrenaline from the break in, but I added, "She's a cat."

If the woman thought this was a strange answer, she didn't show it. "I'm Doctor Alvarez. This way, please."

We followed the doctor down the hallway, and for some reason I felt the need to explain why the vet hadn't met me before. "Mr. Ferguson couldn't make it," I said once inside the exam room. "I'm his fiancé."

Dr. Alvarez nodded. "He's told me about you. Philby is quite a character. It's nice to meet you at last." She took the cat from the carrier. Martini woke up and began to purr.

"She's gotten bigger!" the vet said as she poked the kitten's belly. "And appears to be very well fed."

"Pardon my ignorance," I said. "But what is she here for, exactly?"

I probably should've asked Rex, but figured (and hoped) the vet knew what was going on.

"Just her yearly shots. She's going to need a teeth-cleaning soon. We can make that appointment on your way out."

"Right." I nodded as if I knew what she was talking about.

Dr. Alvarez gave me a look, and I stopped talking. "How's Philby doing? Last time she was here I told Mr. Ferguson to put her on a diet."

I decided not to tell her about Philby's girth. "She's fine. Looks great," I lied.

"Well, Martini here is starting to follow in her mother's footsteps. You might want to put her on a diet soon too."

The vet poked and prodded some more, even pulling open the little cat's mouth and exposed her gums, which made it look like Martini was hate-smiling. She went to the door and called out for someone named Kate, then looked at me apologetically.

"Sorry about that. I forget that Kate isn't here. She's been missing for a few days."

That seemed like a strange thing to say. "Missing? Like milk carton missing?"

She frowned and bit her lip. "I hope not. She just hasn't come in for work or answered her phone."

People didn't usually go missing from small towns. Since everyone knew everyone else, if you were five seconds late for a meeting, the word went out.

"Have you told the police?"

She cocked her head to one side. "Not yet. Do you think we should?"

I shrugged. "Has she done this before?"

"I don't think so. But I've only been working here a few months. I moved here from Truth or Consequences, New Mexico."

"From Truth or Consequences to Who's There, eh? Have you heard about our little rivalry?" Albeit, it was a rivalry that T or C, NM didn't know about—but every Whovian did.

She laughed. "I heard that story on the first day I arrived. Funny, isn't it?"

"Well, I'll call the police station and report it, if you think that's best."

I nodded to indicate that I did. "You should call Rex…Detective Ferguson…directly. He'd want to know."

A young woman came in with a vial and a hypodermic, and I braced for the flurry of fits that Philby had the first time I'd taken her to get shots. Martini gave the vet a disinterested look and fell asleep as the needle went in. What was with this cat?

"She seems healthy and happy," Dr. Alvarez said. "See you in a month."

I gathered up the leash and walked out the door. "Absolutely."

On my way out, I paid for the exam and scheduled the appointment. I felt like such an adult that I skipped out to the car. Until I checked my watch. I only had five minutes before my appointment with Susan! What was I going to do with Martini?

"Ms. Wrath!" A tall brunette with a fauxhawk walked around the desk to shake my hand. She stopped to stare into the cat carrier. "I didn't realize your anxiety was so bad that you adopted a therapy cat."

I looked guiltily at Martini. "Yes, that's right. She's my therapy cat."

I couldn't very well tell her I'd brought a kitten into the hospital so I wouldn't have to drop her off at home.

"She's adorable. Looks a little like Elvis." She went back to her desk and slid a photo across the desk of what looked to be four to six basset hounds passed out on top of each other. "I'm a basset person, myself. Sit down. Please." She motioned to the open chair, and I sat.

"So, tell me how I can help." She sat back and smiled. I liked her immediately.

"Well, I guess…I mean…people tell me I'm freaking out over my upcoming wedding. I've had insomnia for months now."

The therapist nodded like this was the most normal thing ever. "When's the wedding?"

"December 15th. Right around the corner."

Susan smiled. "It must seem like that. But try to take it month by month. You've still got nine months to go."

I hadn't thought of it like that. I felt a little lighter.

"Why don't you tell me a little bit about yourself?" she asked, steepling her fingers. She looked very therapisty doing that.

"Oh. Um…" I hesitated.

Should I tell her about my work at the CIA? Were there patient/doctor privacy rules? How did that work, exactly? The psychologist at the Agency just sent Dan the Ferret Man home and no one ever heard from him again. But my home was here.

"Everything you say here is completely confidential. Bearing that in mind, you don't have to tell me anything you don't want to."

Since I didn't know the woman, and I was a former spy, I decided to err on the side of paranoia.

"I had a wonderful job that I loved. One that took me overseas a lot. But something happened, and I had to leave that job and move back here."

Susan smiled, and I felt myself relax. "What do you do now?"

I shrugged. "I'm a Girl Scout leader."

She leaned forward. "Full-time?"

"No. It's just a volunteer thing. I don't work other than that."

Susan wrote some things down on a notepad. "How long have you known your fiancé?"

"He moved in across the street. We kind of met when dead bodies started popping up around me."

If that concerned her, she didn't show it. I really, really liked her.

One eyebrow went up, but she left my statement alone. "How long did you date before you got engaged?"

"A year, I think. Maybe two. Wait, is that bad that I don't know exactly?" This was starting to feel like a test, and I wanted to pass.

"Not at all." She wrote some more. "I can understand your concerns. Your whole career was stripped from you unexpectedly. You lost something you loved and had to come back to the town you left, probably to find that very adventure."

It was like I was a giant balloon and someone popped me.

"Yes! Yes! That's exactly what happened!"

"Are you thinking someday you'd like to go back to your old job? Leave all of this behind you?"

That stopped me in my tracks. "I guess so. I really miss it. But it will never happen."

There were alternatives. I'd heard about other spies changing to work for the Israeli Mossad among others. Some went to work for the Department of Homeland Security or, in extreme cases, PBS.

"And would your fiancé go with you, or would he stay here?"

"I don't think he'd go with me. He's pretty happy here. But I'd jump at another chance..." Wait! What? Is that what I wanted?

"It's possible that you think, deep down, that the wedding might be a mistake because if given the chance, you'd go back into the field and your fiancé would want to stay here." Susan held up her hands. "Don't take that as gospel. We are just getting started."

Whoa. "Could it really be that simple?"

Susan shook her head. "I don't know. There might be other factors involved. Your insomnia could come from a variety of fears, and that's just one of them."

"What else could it be?"

The counselor smiled, making me relax. "Unresolved issues from your past...problems in past relationships...enjoying the single life...or committing to one man for the rest of your life..."

I went so still I could barely breathe. If she was right, my life was a complete mess. And now that I knew that, it seemed worse. Was I running away from all of that?

"Anyway," Susan said as she stood up, "we can discuss this more next time. I only had thirty minutes free when Mrs. Albers called."

I jumped to my feet. Martini slept on. "You want to see me again? Really?"

She nodded. "If you want to continue on with me, I'm happy to keep working with you. I just have to pencil you in."

"How about tomorrow?" I asked eagerly.

Susan consulted her planner. "The earliest I can get you in is two days from now. I have a client who has decided not to continue working with me. You can have her slot."

"You had a client who dumped you?" What idiot would do that? This was the best thing ever, and in a matter of minutes, she'd figured me out.

"I can't discuss it, but yes. I did. It happens."

Susan escorted Martini and me to the door, shook my hand, and waved me out. I wasn't too surprised to see Kelly in the hallway, waiting for me.

"She's great! How come I didn't know about her sooner? She nailed it!" I gushed.

Kelly grinned. "Susan is one of the best out there."

"Did you know she had a client dump her? What kind of nitwit does that?"

My best friend cocked her head to one side. "I did hear something about that. Not from Susan. But whoever it was disappeared into thin air. Didn't even call to cancel her appointments. Strange, right?"

"That is bizarre." But I didn't really care because that woman's loss was my gain.

That's when Kelly noticed the cat. "Why is she here? You do know you can't have a cat inside a hospital, don't you?" she whispered.

"Oh." I looked down at the kitten, who opened one eye and decided it wasn't worth waking up for. "I told her she's my anxiety cat. I think she bought it."

"Merry…" Kelly warned.

"We had a vet appointment that ran a little long. I couldn't leave her in the car. That would be abuse."

Kelly rolled her eyes and pointed at the doors. With a sigh I made sure my best friend heard, I made my way slowly toward the doors and out into the parking lot.

We made it home within minutes. To my complete surprise, Rex was waiting for me inside my house.

"How did it go?" He took the carrier from me and pulled the little cat out.

Martini licked Rex's hand before he set her down. She bounced off to find Philby.

Should I tell Rex what was going on? Would he think it weird of me to see a counselor?

"Merry?"

"Kelly set me up with a therapist at the hospital."

"You took Martini?"

"I couldn't just leave her in the car…"

He looked at me for a moment. "I'm glad you went."

Did he mean to the vet or…wait! Did Rex think I was crazy?

"You've been dealing with a lot over the past couple of years—losing your job, your partner—Riley and your friend, Maria." He smiled. "This is a good thing."

"I'm glad you think so." I hugged him. "Because I have another appointment soon. I guess one of her clients just dropped off the face of the earth." My mouth was on full autopilot. "Which is weird, because at the vet's office, they told me one of their employees…named Kate, has disappeared also."

Rex clenched his jaw. "Dr. Alvarez called me after you left. It's good you told her to call me."

I knew that look. That was the *I'm not telling you anything and stay out of it* look.

"You don't think this Kate is the same client who ditched Susan, do you?"

He arched one eyebrow. "I'll look into it. Of course, it would be you who finds this out and puts it together."

I couldn't help it. Snooping around crimes was becoming a full-time job for me. But I wasn't going to tell him that.

I decided to change the subject before he ordered me to stay out of it. "What happened with your fire?"

Rex sighed. "We think it was an electrical short. The fire inspector is there right now. I'm going to run home, grab a bite, and head back to the station."

He pulled me against him, and I kissed him and said goodbye. When the door closed behind him, I slumped onto the couch.

Several days of uneven sleep, sneaking around the neighbors' house, and having my head shrunk had taken its toll. Even though it was still early, I climbed into bed with the two cats and wondered why I hadn't come up with the reasons the therapist had.

Was it really about losing my job? I'd thought up until now that this was about getting married. What if it wasn't? And what if I could go back? Would I? Would Rex go with me, or would we have to break up?

My stomach churned at the thought of losing Rex. And the room did this spinning thing I didn't like. *Calm down!* There was no way I could go back into the field. I'd been exposed. To the world. No matter how I disguised myself, there would always be a risk.

Now I really was sad. Susan was right. I hadn't even recognized that this was an issue. Maybe all these investigations I'd been tangled up in since I'd moved back was one way of coping. Rex would love it if I stopped chasing down clues, but it was my nature to do so.

Another thought popped into my mind. Once we were married, would Rex make it his mission to keep me out of his cases?

A little dark storm cloud settled over my thoughts as I tossed and turned the rest of the night, wondering if I was doing the right thing.

CHAPTER ELEVEN

———

I had the strangest dream. I was at a huge community picnic, and there was this epic tug-o-war contest. On one side was Rex, Kelly, her baby Finn (who was surprisingly strong), and my troop. On the other was Riley, the CIA, and a large hairy man dressed as a woman from the 1950s.

I was the rope.

Something was buzzing…my eyes flew open and spotted my cell. The call was from Ferguson Taxidermy.

"Merry! Great!" Randi chirped. "I've got something for you. Come over as soon as you're ready!" She hung up before I could answer.

It was 7 a.m. I'd barely slept. I'd probably snap like Dan the Ferret Man. Kelly had said something about a sleep study, but I couldn't put my finger on what it was. As I moved through my routine of shower, breakfast, and teeth brushing, it felt like I was forgetting something.

The cats were not pleased that I was leaving. I don't know why, because I fed them. Ungrateful beasts.

I made it to the shop within half an hour of Randi's call. What kind of dead animal thing did she have in store for me today? The shotgun sound went off as I walked through the door, but I managed to look like it didn't surprise me this time. Randi was standing there, waiting for me, as she held something behind her back.

"I think you'll love this!" She practically levitated with glee as she handed me a dead bird.

"It's a brooch! You need something blue for the wedding, so I stuffed a blue jay!"

I stared at the thing. As a brooch, it would take up a quarter of the body of my wedding gown. The blue jay's wings were fully extended, flattening him somewhat. It kind of looked like someone had stepped on him in mid-flight.

Randi took my silence for appreciation. "Isn't it fabulous? I'm going to make one attached to a top hat for Rex."

I laughed out loud. "I'd like to see Rex in a top hat. I doubt he'll wear it."

For the first time since I'd met her, Randi frowned. "It's a tradition in the Ferguson family that the man must wear a top hat and tails for his wedding. I hope he remembers that when he orders his tuxedo. Maybe I should order the hat for him."

"You have wedding traditions?" My family didn't have wedding traditions. In fact, I couldn't think of *any* family traditions. It would be nice to be part of a family that did things a certain way.

She nodded as she stepped forward and proceeded to pin the monstrosity onto my sweatshirt.

"Several. Our ancestors were very big on tradition."

"Oh. Well, we don't have any that I can think of."

Randi continued as if she hadn't heard me. "And we are Scottish on our father's side. So we have a lot of ideas on how weddings should be organized."

I wracked my brain to think if I'd ever heard of the Scots having a culture that embraced using dead animals as accessories.

"Some of the traditions"—Randi kept talking—"are optional, such as the sword fight between the bride and groom and the caber toss. Others are mandatory, including the top hat and the bride feeding baklava to the minister before the vows."

"Why do I have to feed baklava to the minister?" I asked, but was really wondering if I got to eat it too. I loved baklava.

"It's to signify the bride's culinary skills. But it can be replaced by you stepping on a haggis."

I shuddered. I did not like haggis. Sheep intestines stuffed with sausage into a sheep's stomach. There was no way I wanted to do that. But if Randi knew that my culinary skills involved a can opener and microwaveable food, I might not have a choice.

"I'll never remember that. Can you make me a list?"

Randi nodded enthusiastically. "Absolutely! So, you love the brooch? Because if not, I am working on a handbag made from a sloth for something new. Or, I could loan you our grandmother's lizard tail ring for something borrowed."

I really wanted to see the lizard tail ring, but the sloth bag was out of the question. "Let me think about it. Maybe I should bounce this off Rex."

That seemed like a safe bet. Although, the lizard tail ring was probably a lot smaller than the blue jay brooch. I looked down, and could swear it was staring right at me.

"Hey!" Ronni shouted, appearing as if out of thin air. "That woman still hasn't picked up or paid for her order!"

Randi stepped back, a look of alarm on her face. "She hasn't? Have you tried calling her?"

Ronni stomped her foot like a toddler in a tantrum. "She's not answering."

Suddenly, I wanted to help. I didn't know how, but maybe as a gesture of good will toward my new family, I could do something. "What did she have done?"

Randi reached behind a counter and pulled out a cat on top of a Roomba. The cat was smiling and had a dead mouse in its mouth.

"Is it attached to the robot vacuum?" I asked.

Ronni barked, "Well of course it is! I had the worst time doing that without damaging the machine. She wants it to still work."

Randi grinned at the device. "Mr. Pickles will be cleaning her floors forever. Isn't that nice?"

"Not if Kate Becks doesn't pick it up!" Ronni snatched the thing from her twin.

I felt a little prickle in my throat. "Did you say her first name is Kate?" I asked.

Ronni scowled. "Yeah. So?"

My mind worked furiously. "I think I know her. Do you have an address for her? I could stop by and remind her."

I did not know Kate Becks, but she had to be the woman the vet said was missing and who didn't show up for a session with Susan!

"Why would you do that?" Ronni barked.

"Now, Ronni," Randi said softly, "I think that's nice." She left the room and returned with an address on a Post-it note. "Thanks for doing this, Merry!"

"No problem." I looked at the dead blue jay pinned to my chest. "Thanks for the brooch. It's, um, awesome!"

I got out of there as fast as I could without being rude. Once in the car, I studied the address. Huh. Kate lived only a couple of streets over from me. Not that that was unusual. Not in a small town.

The pieces flew together in my mind. Kate, the vet tech who was seeing a therapist, was missing. An idea popped into my head. The Fontanas were seen (by me) carrying a body. Was that Kate Becks? If I hadn't been driving, I'd have clapped my hands together.

The address led me to a small craftsman-style house with a huge porch. I pulled up on the street, several houses down, instead of in the driveway. If this was a different Kate, I didn't want to scare her. If it was the missing woman, I didn't want Rex to drive by and see my van in the driveway.

And if he did, I was legitimately here on an errand for his sisters. I kept this in mind as I walked up to the front door. The porch was littered with half a dozen newspapers, and her mailbox was overflowing. That was not a good sign. Yay!

Why didn't the paperboy or mailman call this in? Maybe they thought she'd gone on a vacation and forgot to tell the newspaper or post office? In any event, it didn't stop them from delivering more mail and newspapers. That's just plain lazy.

My body blocked the view of the door and mailbox. With my left hand I knocked, while I ran my right hand through the envelopes in the mailbox, glancing through them. It was the usual. Bills for electricity and cable…a couple of sales ads from the local grocery store…things like that. Nothing stood out as odd.

I knocked again, a little louder this time. "Miss Becks?" I called out. "I'm from Ferguson Taxidermy. Your order is ready for pickup."

If anyone was watching me, they'd just think I was here on a routine business call, wearing a giant dead bird on my shirt. For a moment I thought about taking it off, but it seemed like an advertisement for the twins' business (and I had no idea what else to do with it since I was away from the van).

Still, no answer. I didn't hear or see anyone else out and about. I took a tissue from my pocket and, covering the doorknob, gently turned.

The door opened. It was unlocked.

"Thanks for letting me in," I shouted for anyone who was watching. "I'd love a glass of lemonade!" I added as I walked inside and closed the door behind me.

The living room had been totally ransacked. The couch and a wingback chair had been ripped apart. A stand with drawers had been knocked over, and each drawer lay on the floor, empty. A large painting sat on the couch, its glass shattered.

Several holes had been punched in the wall. Someone must've been looking for a safe. Did they find it? I walked through the house. Each room was the same. Complete chaos and broken furniture. Whoever had been here had gone through every inch of this house and, by the amount of damage, had had a tough time finding what they wanted.

On a dresser in the bedroom, I found a picture of Mr. Pickles, the living version of the cat I'd just seen at Randi's. The cat looked like he hated everything—much worse than he did dead. This was a cat only the owner could love. Using my cell phone, I snapped a picture of the photo and moved back through the house to see if I'd missed a study or den.

I had. It threw me because I'd originally thought it a guest room, since it had a bed in it. A guest room that seemed to double for an office. Against the far wall was a huge, very expensive computer monitor with a broken screen, lying on its side. The keyboard was in once piece, but the computer looked like it had been ripped off of the desk.

The room was littered with file folders and paper, like a tree had lost its leaves. I sifted through a few pages with a tissue so as not to leave fingerprints.

All I found were phone bills. A lot of phone bills. I took a few pictures of the ones on top, when I noticed a squad car pulling into the driveway.

Oh no.

The doors opened, and I watched as Rex and Kevin Dooley walked up to the front door. It was unlocked because I'd left it that way. And my car was on the street! The thing that probably saved me was it was a generic-looking silver minivan with regular plate. Rex didn't appear to notice, because now he was stepping onto the porch.

This was not going to make my fiancé very happy. Yes, technically I was there to help his sisters. Rex wouldn't see it that way.

Looking around the room, I noticed a closet. No good. If he was searching the place, he'd look there first. I heard footsteps as the two men walked into the house. Going out the window would be noticed by neighbors who were probably glued to their windows since a police cruiser was in the driveway.

There was only one way out, through the door and down the hallway that emptied into the living room. The living room where the detective and Officer Dooley now stood. That wasn't going to work.

If I didn't hide in the closet, that left two spots—under the bed and behind the desk. The bed was another place they'd look. Even the desk would get their attention. But it had a high-backed topper and was a few feet away from the wall. While the odds were good they'd check out the desk, they were very slightly slimmer they'd look behind it.

I heard the men talking about the mess in the living room. Rex suggested they investigate the rest of the rooms. I dove behind the desk and drew myself up into a ball.

It was remarkably clean for a place like this. At my house, there'd be a million cat toys and enough cat hair to make another whole cat. I once moved the sofa and found fifty-four catnip mice I didn't even know I had.

Rex and Kevin were in the main bedroom now, searching it. They talked about the closet, under the bed, all those things. I was doomed. Perhaps I should prepare a statement now.

I came here for your sisters and thought I heard someone call me in and fell behind this desk...

Next, the men checked the bathroom, which was between the two rooms. I heard the shower curtain slide, but that was pretty much all they'd be able to search. The bathroom was small. In a matter of seconds, they'd be here.

Why was there such a huge gap between the desk and the wall? It didn't make sense really. This room wasn't huge, and shoving it up against the wall would give up a few feet of floor space.

That's when I noticed a cord that didn't look like the others. This particular computer and monitor had black cords. But sitting there, tangled in all the others, was a white cord. I grabbed one end and tugged to determine what it went to.

A small door opened up in the paneling. A way out! I scrambled through the doorway and closed it from the inside. Saved! I doubted Rex would notice the cords. It was very dark in the passageway. I took one step, and my foot gave way to empty air. I fell about six feet and landed on a pillow.

Fortunately, I didn't cry out. It's a totally natural reaction, but as a spy I'd learned to control that response. I lay there in the darkness, being thankful for the pillow, and listened. There was no sound indicating that above me, two men were searching a room.

Soundproof? And obviously light proof. I turned on the flashlight app on my cell and held it up around me. The room I was in was tiny. It must be part of the basement, but there was no door. The only way out was through the passage above me.

A light switch was on the wall directly in front. Since there were no windows, and no light leaking from the room above, I switched it on.

The secret room was completely empty except for the pillow and a tiny table with someone sitting at it, their back to me. I froze. It looked like a man, but I couldn't be sure. If he'd heard me land or was startled by the light coming on, he didn't show it. Was he dead?

Having nothing for a weapon, I grabbed the pillow. Maybe I could startle him with it somehow.

"Excuse me?" I whispered.

The man didn't move. Definitely dead. I swallowed hard and skirted the perimeter of the room to stay out of his reach in case he was alive.

It was a dummy. A life-sized, naked dummy. More like a mannequin really. The body was stiff like plaster, and the face was mostly lifelike. A blond patch of hair stood up in a spiked hairdo.

The naked dummy stared ahead, smiling vacantly at the wall. Who puts a naked mannequin in a secret room? Why not put clothes on him? A quick glance I wasn't proud of told me that unlike department store mannequin, this one was anatomically correct. Enthusiastically so. Ewww.

Stuffing the pillow over the dummy's groin, I stepped closer to check out the setup. The table had a laptop, a shortwave radio, a small ream of white paper, and a mason jar filled with yellow liquid. I unscrewed the lid and sniffed. Lemon juice!

There was only one reason to have a hidden lair, a shortwave radio, and lemon juice (unlike the naked dummy— which there was no reason for). It could only mean one thing.

Kate Becks was a spy.

CHAPTER TWELVE

————

As badly as I wanted to, I couldn't turn on the shortwave radio or the computer without making a sound. And while I couldn't hear the men upstairs, they still might be able to hear me. Which presented another dilemma—how would I know when to leave?

I couldn't very well pop up through the secret door. My presence was unnoticed so far. I examined the six-foot drop over the pillow. On the wall there was a bookshelf built into the drywall. Only, this bookshelf didn't have any books.

A built-in ladder! Okay, so when the time came, I had a way out. But when would the time come?

My guess was that forensics was upstairs or would be there momentarily, going over everything with a fine-tooth comb. From my experience with Rex, I also knew that would take a long time. And when finished, they would post a guard at the front and back doors.

I hadn't made it to the other exit, but I was guessing that it was, like many houses of this type, in the kitchen.

I listed my problems. Number one—how would I know when they were finished? Number two—how would I get out unnoticed? And number three—I was hungry. A quick search of my purse found something called a protein bar. Rex had started working out at the local Y, saying he wanted to look good for the wedding.

I'd told him he already was perfect, but he'd insisted on going and had asked me to go too. After I'd stopped laughing, I'd discovered he was serious. Then he'd handed me this protein bar, and I'd chucked it into my purse.

It tasted like a piece of cardboard, layered with sandpaper with glued on pencil erasers. But it was all I had, and you learned quickly as a spy to eat what's on hand, because you had no idea when you'd eat next. I've eaten moldy tomatoes in Bulgaria, a decade old can of baked beans in Sri Lanka, stir-fried bugs in China, and worst of the worst, fifteen pair of wax lips at a novelty warehouse in Portugal. To this day, I can't even look at a candle.

Finishing the protein bar, I carefully picked up the crumbs that had fallen and stuffed them and the wrapper into my purse. That problem was now solved.

According to my phone, I'd been hiding out for an hour. Was that enough time? A thought came to me, and I texted Kelly.

Five minutes later, she responded, telling me she had taken Finn for a walk in her stroller, and yes there were still police cars there. She also mentioned she was worried about me, which was nice.

I told her where the spare car keys were in my house and asked her to take my car back home. Fortunately, Kelly didn't live far from me, so this wouldn't take too long.

She texted back ten minutes later that the deal was done and she didn't think Rex had noticed.

At least there was that.

I had time to kill, so I attempted to google Kate Becks on my phone. All I found was a Facebook page where, through dozens of pictures of a hostile Mr. Pickles, she posted about her cat, and her work at the vet, and a story about her in the vet's newsletter. She'd made Cat Lady of the Month fifteen times.

At least now I suspected that the Fontanas had killed Kate Becks, for whatever reason, but something to do with them both being spies. And illegals at that. While I did a victory dance in my head, I knew that wouldn't be enough to convince the police.

Kevin hadn't found a dead person, and neither had I. All the evidence I had about the Fontanas was circumstantial. Granted, it was based on my years of experience with the CIA. But that wouldn't hold up on an arrest warrant. I'd need more to prove I was right.

The biggest question was, why were there three illegals in Who's There, Iowa? This town of five thousand wasn't exactly a seething terrorist hotbed. The closest thing to a sleeper cell would be my Girl Scout troop. And they weren't quite there…yet.

What was worth spying on here? Des Moines was a large city and only thirty minutes away, but there wasn't much espionage worthy there unless you thought insurance companies and *Better Homes & Gardens* magazine were scary.

I could take the laptop. Rex might not realize it wasn't mine. Unless he examined it, he wouldn't know it was Kate's. The Fontanas hadn't gotten it because they didn't know it was even here. I'd be saving the day, really.

Something heavy fell onto the floor above me. Okay, not totally soundproof. The sound came from near the computer desk. It was possible the forensics team would find the secret door. I snatched the pillow from the naked dummy's crotch and made my way to the other side of the little table, where I switched off the light. Curling up in a ball, my head on the pillow, I waited. In total darkness.

I woke up with a start. How long had I been out? I checked my cell. Four hours? It had to be the insomnia. My sleep-deprived brain, when plunged into a sensory-deprived setting, had shut down.

According to my cell, it was two in the afternoon. My stomach complained audibly. The police had to be gone by now, right? I moved toward the ladder/bookcase, climbed, and very quietly opened the door just a crack.

A pair of feet wearing sport sandals, facing the other way, caused me to close the door. Someone was still here.

But why was a policeman wearing sandals? That didn't make sense. They wore black dress shoes. But then, maybe the forensics team wears them. And since I didn't know for sure, I couldn't rule out that they were still here.

Why were they still here? Then I remembered the reams of pages scattered about the room above. Okay, so it would take a while to clean that mess up. They'd have to go through each and every page.

After lowering myself back down to the floor, I unplugged the laptop and stuffed it and the cord into my purse. Fortunately, I carry a large tote bag as a purse. Granted, it's a canvas bag from the grocery store, but to me it's a purse.

I used to carry the smallest handbag I could find. All I needed was room for my wallet and cell. But then I realized if I carried a large purse, I could keep everything I might ever need in there. If you looked inside my bag right now, you'd find Band-Aids, tissues, a lighter (for starting fires, of course), my spy camera—which I don't use now that I have a smartphone, fifteen packs of gum (trust me on this—you can't give some to one girl without providing enough for the whole troop), five knives of various sizes, and a book about Australian water fowl that I found in the library.

Something dripped down onto my hand. It came from the ceiling, and I realized I was just under the door. I switched off the lights to reveal a tiny sliver of light overhead. I hadn't shut the door all the way.

Drip.

Another tiny droplet landed on my hand. How did it get wet upstairs? I sniffed the liquid and immediately started to panic. Kerosene. And then I smelled the tiniest whiff of smoke.

That wasn't the police upstairs. They don't usually pour kerosene on a crime scene and light it. Except in Colombia. That's kind of a thing there.

Whoever trashed the rooms above was trying to destroy their handiwork. How could they do that with the police standing guard outside?

Unless, there weren't any officers standing guard. More likely it was Kevin in a squad car across the street with his arm wrist-deep in a bag of fried pork rinds.

It didn't matter, because I was going to be burned alive unless I got out of here somehow. And fast.

I took a chance, hoping the arsonists had torched the room and fled. Scaling the bookshelf once more, I popped open the door to see the floor in a sea of flames. All that paper was excellent kindling.

So now I was in a room saturated with paper and giant, scary flames. Running across the floor would only make me splash kerosene on myself, causing anything exposed to flame to catch fire. I scaled the back of the desk and climbed over to the front. From there, I jumped onto the bed, then to the doorway.

The floor in the hallway was dry. Maybe they thought they could start the fire in one room and it would spread that way. But why pick a room with a window that faces front?

I didn't have time to think about that. Racing through the living room, I made it out the back way through the kitchen and kept running until I was two blocks away.

Sirens erupted in the distance, and soon two fire trucks passed me. I ducked into an alley and took the long way around the fire until I got to my house. The cats weren't there to greet me, but that was okay. I hit the shower, washing the smell of kerosene and smoke off me. Then I took my clothes downstairs and threw them in the washer.

I couldn't do much about my shoes or the scorched and now broken blue jay, so I stashed those outside in the backyard. Hopefully they'd air out. It took all of twenty minutes to do this. Soon I was on my couch, wearing clean sweats and rubber gloves, and going through the stolen laptop. I kept an eye on the window in case Rex came by, but I was pretty sure he was at the crime scene.

If the fire razed the house, I was pretty sure the secret room would be discovered. They might find the remains of the radio and lemon juice, but chances were they'd be destroyed too.

The laptop came on, but I was blocked. I needed a password. I tried Kate's name, her address, *Mr. Pickles* again, and even *Naked Dummy*, but nothing worked. I needed a hacker. Unfortunately, I was so distracted, I barely noticed my front door opening.

"Howdy, ma'am." A man in a hard hat and coveralls stood in my doorway as I jumped to my feet and shoved the laptop behind the couch. "I need to check your meter," the man wearing a huge moustache said. He sounded like a cowboy. He looked like Riley.

"Dammit, Riley!" I swore. "You can't walk in here anytime you want!"

He closed the door behind him and took off the hat. "Sure I can. You gave me a key, remember?"

I grabbed his wrist and twisted it hard, snatching the key from his hand.

"No, you made a copy of the key that I took back from you last time. Why are you here, and why do you look like the saddest member of the Village People?"

Riley peeled off the mustache. "I can't fool you, can I?"

"Again," I insisted, "why are you here, and why are you in disguise?"

He shrugged. "No reason. I was just passing through from—"

"Chicago to Omaha?" I asked. "I don't think so. For one thing, why travel incognito? Secondly, we're about thirty minutes off Highway 80, so this is a detour. Why?"

He sighed and unzipped the coveralls to reveal a very fitted white T-shirt and jeans. Riley sat down on the couch and patted the seat beside him. I sat in a chair instead. Riley had a strange effect on me. I wasn't immune to his charms. We'd been a couple once, and it was hard to forget.

"The truth is"—he ran his hands through his thick golden hair—"I'm on a case."

Was he investigating the Fontanas? Kate Becks? I really was on to something! I just couldn't let him know that.

"Here? In Who's There? What kind of case could you be on here?"

He grinned. "That's confidential."

I wanted to murder him.

"Seriously? You've come to see me twice. That means you want to tell me."

A very naughty look crossed his face. "Well, you could always seduce it out of me."

"That"—I folded my arms over my chest to show him I meant it—"is not happening. You should just tell me. Out of professional courtesy."

"Where are the cats?" He looked around.

"Don't change the subject…"

"No, really Wrath." He stood up and looked around. "Where are Philby and Martini?"

"What are you talking about? They're...somewhere...doing cat things."

It was weird that the cats didn't tackle Riley the minute he appeared. I started down the hallway after a glance into the kitchen. The cats were curled up in my unmade bed.

Riley stood dangerously close behind me. "So, they're in *bed.*"

Only, he said the word *bed* as if it was a suggestion. I broke free and turned to face him. Philby and Martini woke up and stretched. Upon seeing my former handler, they threw themselves at him, purring. He had no choice but to scoop them up and carry them back down the hall to the living room, where once again, he sat on the couch.

"Lighten up, Wrath," he said. "You're so tense. You never used to be this tense. Is something bothering you?"

He was talking about the wedding.

"Yes," I said airily, "my old boss keeps showing up in disguise for no apparent reason."

"You're off the payroll," he said. "I don't have to tell you anything."

"I could torture it out of you," I warned.

"I'm not sure we have time for foreplay." He winked.

I screamed in frustration. This man was driving me insane!

"Sorry," Riley said with eyes that didn't mean it. "I took that too far."

I said nothing as I went to the kitchen, pulled a salami log and cheddar cheese from the fridge, and started chopping it up. Riley joined me and poured us each a glass of red wine. I tried to give the impression that slicing the salami was something I was going to do to him if he didn't talk. He ignored me.

Philby jumped up onto the counter. She touched the first slice with her paw, then sat back. It was an old trick of hers—one she usually reserved for bacon. The cat knew if she touched something, like the burger or whatever I was eating, I'd give it to her, knowing those paws had been in a litter box.

I handed her the slice of meat, and she began devouring it. Martini stayed on the floor, rubbing up against Riley's ankles.

That was good because she needed to maintain a healthy weight until I saw the vet again. Philby was a lost cause.

After munching on a few slices of cheese and meat, I asked as casually as possible, "Are you here because of my neighbors?"

He didn't even blink. "What about your neighbors?"

"The Fontanas," I said at last. I didn't like tipping my hand. "Are you watching them because they're illegals?"

Riley looked me in the eye. "Honestly, Merry, I have no idea what you're talking about."

I threw my hands in the air. "What is it then? Why are you here?"

He said nothing for a few minutes.

"Okay," Riley said slowly, "suppose I was here for a reason. What makes you think it has anything to do with you? It isn't all about you."

"Then why are you in my house, and what is that reason? Remember, I'm holding a salami knife."

I'd just recently learned that knives had names, so yes, I was showing off a bit. I had no idea if there was such a thing as a salami knife, but maybe Riley wouldn't know that.

He leaned back in his chair at the breakfast bar. "I'm here to visit my goddaughter, Finn."

I shook my head. "No, you are not."

"What makes you so sure? It's not strange to imagine I would take a small detour to see the child I'm responsible for."

"And does Finn, who's only a year and a half old, require you to dress like an outrageously handsome meter reader when you come visit her?"

I slapped my hand over my mouth. I didn't mean to say that.

Riley laughed. "Okay, okay. I am looking into something. But I can't tell you anything about it."

I ignored the last sentence. "So, it is the Fontanas. Or is it Kate Becks? Or both?"

He shook his head. "Where do you get your imagination?" Riley stood up and put his disguise back on.

"Maybe because I only see you in disguise anymore?" I asked as I followed him to the door.

Before I could react, he pulled me into his arms and kissed me. Everything went limp, except for my rage, which I used to pull away from him.

I stood there, fuming and sexually confused, unable to speak.

"Bye Wrath." He winked. "Say hi to Rex for me."

He's lucky I left the salami knife in the kitchen, I thought as the door closed behind him.

CHAPTER THIRTEEN

———

I fumed for hours, stomping around the house, slamming doors, and shouting at myself. The cats followed me from room to room, waiting to see what I'd do next. Maybe they were worried about me. Maybe they were entertained. It was hard to tell at that point because my fury was burning through my lips.

He'd kissed *me*! I didn't kiss him. And it was a good kiss. Dammit! I grabbed the salami knife and threw it, scoring a perfect bull's-eye in the target I had pinned to one of the cupboards. I'd never really liked the wood, but Kelly had told me they were fine and I should wait until they wore out to replace them.

I put the target up the next day. She didn't say I couldn't give the wood a little help...

Whether he was in town for work or not, one thing was clear. Riley was messing with me. Who kisses an engaged woman? While I didn't know much about marriage rituals, I was pretty sure kissing the bride-to-be was something only done by the groom-to-be.

The question was, was Riley just trying to make me mad, or did he have feelings for me? No. It didn't matter how he felt. I was engaged to Rex. Happily. I wanted to marry Rex. Riley was fun, but he wasn't what I wanted. Rex was a grown-up. He was sweet, and smart, loved my cats, and made me tingle when he kissed me.

Unfortunately, Riley's kiss had the same effect.

Arghhhhhh!

I threw a fork this time, and the tines straddled the salami knife on the target. This was so maddening! I had enough on my plate without…without Riley stirring the pot! I'd definitely need to talk to Susan about this.

I definitely wouldn't be talking to Rex or Kelly about this.

It didn't matter anyway. If Riley told people he'd kissed me, I'd just deny it. I was an excellent liar. And then, I'd remove his liver with a fork. In fact, next time I saw him I'd…I'd…well, I don't know what I'd do, but he wouldn't like it.

Eventually, I ran out of steam, and cutlery, and fell onto the sofa to pout. Martini sprawled out on the back of the sofa, belly up. Philby stood by my feet and stared at something behind the couch.

"What is it?" I asked. "Don't tell me we have mice now."

I got up and followed her gaze to find Kate Becks' laptop! In my blistering, fork-tossing rage, I'd completely forgotten about it. Pulling the computer onto my lap, I turned it on. A background of Mr. Pickles with a sour look filled the screen. Philby hissed at it. I couldn't blame her.

It was password protected. This wasn't a surprise, just a disappointment. Every rare now and then, you get lucky on these things. Sometimes a spy is just lazy and doesn't make a password. Or worse, they use something obvious like 1234.

Unfortunately, Kate wasn't lazy or obvious. I typed in *Mr. Pickles*, the name of the vet clinic, and anything cat themed with no luck. Maybe food would help. In the kitchen I got a jar of peanut butter and a spoon, with a glass of white wine. White wine goes with peanut butter, right?

I sat at the breakfast bar with the laptop until the sky grew dark. I tried all of my tricks, from an electro-magnetic disrupter to calling in a favor to a guy at the NSA who owes me two hundred dollars for cookies, but they didn't work either.

I suspect Marvin was holding out on me. He had access to some serious technology. Well if he thought he was getting any cookies next year, he had another think coming. Maybe I should send Betty to collect.

Finally, I shoved it underneath some wedding magazines for cover, and that's when I remembered I didn't have a dress yet. This was an excellent opportunity for a distraction, so I called

Kelly and asked her to come over. To my surprise, even with the late hour, she agreed.

Five minutes later we were skimming through the magazines. As I filled her in on Randi's alleged traditional requirements.

She laughed. "Let me see the brooch!"

Oh, crap. I ran out to the backyard and, after fighting off a raccoon for it, brought it in and handed it to her.

"The wing is broken." Kelly sounded sad as she turned it over in her hands. "And it smells like kerosene and smoke."

The right wing was broken. Randi would not be happy.

A twinge of guilt the size of the Grand Canyon weighed down on me. "Do you think we can fix it?"

"You're going to wear it?" Kelly asked. "It will hide the bodice of your dress!"

"What dress?" I shoved the magazines away. "None of these are me at all! I'm not exactly the lace or beaded dress type."

All of the dresses we'd found had either voluminous skirts, were strapless with eight million beads, or something terrifying called a "mermaid" style.

"I can't run in this!" I pointed at said mermaid dress.

Kelly rolled her eyes. "Why would you need to run in it? You'll only wear it during the ceremony and reception."

"One should always be prepared. For anything. What if there's a robbery? Or a fire?" It could happen. I've been at weddings in six different time zones, and four of them caught fire. "There've been three fires in the area in the last month."

"Speaking of which"—she ignored me and kept turning pages—"what's up with that? Has Rex said anything?"

I shook my head. "No. I guess we'll just have to wait for the paper." And because of Riley's kiss, I wasn't too keen to press Rex for any information at the moment.

"It's Thursday. And the next one doesn't come out until Saturday."

That was the joy of a small-town newspaper. It only came out on Wednesdays and Saturdays.

"I guess I should ask…" I said absently.

"What's going on?" Kelly closed the magazine and turned her full attention on me. "Did something happen?"

I gave her a look. "Did Riley come see you this afternoon?"

Kelly frowned. "No. Why?"

I filled her in on my two visits. I left out the part about the kiss. I was pretty sure she'd judge me for that. I knew there were rules about getting married, even if I wasn't sure what they were. My best friend listened without speaking. When I finished, she went back to her magazine.

"I knew you had unresolved issues with him."

"What? How do you get that out of what I said? The man has come to me, both times incognito. I'd say he's the one with issues."

Kelly turned a page and tried to act casual. "Have you told Rex about Riley's visits?"

I feigned interest in a particularly ugly neon pink bridal gown with puffy sleeves the size of my head. "No."

Her cautious tone with me seemed out of character. "Doesn't that strike you as lying to him?"

Okay, she was judgy.

"Not necessarily. If the Feds are here working on a case and he doesn't know about it, he'll be angry. I'd hate to do that to him."

While that was technically true, I suspected that if you added "and your fiancé doesn't tell you the Feds are here, he'll be upset," it would be true also.

"Well…" Kelly sighed. "This is none of my business anyway. Let's change the subject. Have you ordered the berets for Thinking Day?"

I ran and grabbed my laptop from the bedroom and quickly typed in *black beret*.

"Why run and get that one, when you could've used this one?" Kelly pointed at the laptop on the table. The one that had been hidden by magazines. Magazines we were now looking through.

"Because," I said as I bought the French hats, "that one isn't mine."

I closed my laptop and told her about Katie Becks and my narrow escape from being turned into one of Betty's blackened hot dogs. That kid had a thing for really, really burnt food. You might think I'm exaggerating, but at the last campout, she blackened a hot dog to the point where it liquefied inside. And she ate it.

Instead of lecturing me on the stupidity of almost dying—a thing she did a lot—Kelly thought for a moment.

"You need a hacker."

I nodded.

Kelly continued, "I know who you can ask."

My jaw dropped open. "Who?" Kelly knew a hacker? How did she know a hacker? My best friend was pretty straightlaced. Especially when I took Martini to the hospital.

"You'll see her at the meeting tomorrow," Kelly said.

One of the girls? I guess that made sense. They were pretty savvy. One time Inez got in trouble for hacking into the school district computer. She didn't even change grades, just changed the lunch menu so they'd have pigs in a blanket every day for a week. The lunch ladies didn't even notice.

Kelly shoved a magazine at me with a very simple gown. White satin, fitted, off the shoulder. I liked it.

"As much as I don't like you involving the girls in espionage, bring the laptop."

"And the dress?" I asked as I tore the page from the magazine.

"Tomorrow morning…" Kelly nodded. "We will go to the bridal shop and see what we can do."

CHAPTER FOURTEEN

———

I didn't sleep at all. Every time I closed my eyes, I thought about Riley's kiss. Oh sure. You probably thought I'd be reliving the terror of almost being burned alive. But I didn't. I'd been in so many life-threatening scenarios as a spy, they hardly registered anymore.

In Paraguay I'd been cornered by a gang of street thugs who'd thought I had drugs on me. In Bucharest, while impersonating the Romanian Secretary of Agriculture, I'd had to give a one-hour, spur of the moment speech to a bunch of farmers on turnip futures. And in Cairo I'd been in a basket that had been set on fire and thrown into a lake.

I always wondered who would set something on fire and then toss it into water. I just chalked it up as being grateful they were that stupid.

Riley's actions were driving me nuts. He was playing games with me, and I didn't like it one bit.

But did I not like it because he was irritating or because, as Kelly suggested, I still had feelings for him? I wracked my brain for hours before getting up and going into the dark garage to watch my neighbors.

Philby joined me. Together we sat there, in the darkness, watching the Fontanas move around behind the blinds. I didn't even care what they were doing. I was more concerned about my own problems.

At six in the morning I took a long shower, downed half a box of Lucky Charms, and sat staring at the wall until it was time to go.

Kelly met me at the bridal shop—A Storybook Ending— at nine in the morning.

"You look terrible," my friend said.

I had to admit, she was right. The purplish bags under my eyes gave me a kind of psycho look.

"I was up all night," was all I said.

"Hi!" A young woman greeted us, wearing a lavender suit. "I'm Betsy...oh my God!" Her eyes grew wide and she froze in place as she stared at me. "Are you okay?" She really did look concerned. I gave her points for that.

"Insomnia," Kelly whispered while twirling her finger around the right side of her head as if to add *and she's crazy too.*

I glared at her. "I'm fine. Let's look at dresses."

Betsy was still staring at my face. "Oh. Um. Right away. Let me guess. You're about a size four?" She ran off, disappearing into the back room.

"Is she supposed to do that?" I pointed in the direction she'd vanished.

"Sit down," Kelly insisted.

She pulled a makeup kit from her purse and started wiping stuff on me. I'm not much for makeup, but I didn't want a lecture either, so I let her torture me. Most of the time I wear mascara and eyeliner, because I think it makes me look more awake. Something that was failing me at this moment.

Then she ran her fingers through my hair, and I flinched.

"Hey! That hurts."

Kelly frowned. "We're going to have to do something about your hair."

"What's wrong with my hair?" I patted it to make sure it was still there.

My short, curly dishwater blonde hair was unruly on the best of days. I kept it short so I wouldn't have to do much with it.

"We could color it..." Kelly nodded. "You used to be a brunette, before you changed to blonde when you moved back here. Maybe we could go with a dark chestnut?"

I scrambled to recall the color of a chestnut. In fact, I wasn't sure I'd ever seen one.

"My stars!" Betsy joined us with a rolling rack full of dresses. "You look so much better!"

I walked over to a mirror. Wow. Kelly had made the bags disappear and evened out my skin tone. She'd also done my brows and lips. Who was this woman in the mirror? How could I get Kelly to come over every morning and do whatever it was?

"We're going to color her hair too," Kelly said. "Dark chestnut."

Betsy agreed. "Good idea. That will look more natural than what she currently has."

I waved my arms. "Hello! I'm right here!" I was not coloring my hair. This was the color I picked when I went from Finn Czrygy to Merry Wrath. I had to draw the line somewhere.

Betsy ignored my outburst. "Now take a look at some of these dresses, and let me know if there's anything you like."

Kelly moved through the rack quickly, arranging the dresses in some sort of order. I let her because she knew what I wanted. When she finished, she held up a dress in a long plastic bag and dragged me off to the dressing room.

A few minutes later I shouted, "You're going to have to come in here and help me. This is impossible!"

Kelly slid through the curtain and began doing up buttons, hooks, and whatever else there was. The dress felt like it weighed forty pounds. The neckline was square, and I liked that. But I didn't like the millions of tiny pearls stitched into the dress.

"The skirt is too bushy," I mumbled.

"Full," Kelly corrected. "The skirt is too *full*. Do you like the bodice?"

I nodded. "I do. But this skirt is way too much. How would I sit down? And I'll be tired after one hour with all this extra weight." I wanted to say I couldn't run in it but decided against that.

"You won't even notice the weight on your wedding day. Trust me. Let's go look in the three-way mirror."

I stomped over to a pedestal, holding what seemed like miles of satin in my arms. I let the dress fall and turned around. Whoa. I liked it. Did I really look like that? That wasn't me.

"In some places," Betsy was telling us, "someone stands in for the bride for to try on the dress so she can see it clearly."

I turned to my best friend with a hopeful look on my face.

"No," was all Kelly had to say.

It took two hours to try on six dresses. Seriously, how did women do this? You couldn't even get dressed or undressed by yourself. Why couldn't I just wear something simple, like a short, regular dress?

And when did I get so picky? I liked the neckline on one dress, the so-called bodice on another, the sleeves on a different dress, and none of the skirts.

"This is hard," I grumbled as I dragged fifty pounds of dress back to the dressing room. One more dress to try on and I was done.

"Quit complaining," Kelly said. "If you had your way, you'd wear an oversize bathrobe and slippers."

I brightened. "That's a great idea!"

"Not if Rex is in tails," Kelly countered. "As your matron of honor, it's my duty to make sure you look okay."

"Matron? Like a prison matron?"

Kelly sighed. "Sometimes that's exactly what it feels like."

I barely looked at the dress as I slipped it off the hanger and over my head. I was just counting down the seconds when I could be free from this…whatever it was.

"That's it! This is the one!" Kelly smiled, dragging me out to the large mirrors.

I stepped up onto the pedestal and stared. She was right. The dress was just like the one in the magazine. A simple satin dress with a portrait color (that's what Betsy said it was), three-quarter-length sleeves, and a no-fuss skirt that wasn't puffed out with itchy crinolines.

"Yes. This is the one." I turned around, to the side, and back again.

Kelly took a picture. "For Judith."

Smart. Mom would love to see it. I probably should have had her come out for this. Would she be upset I hadn't included her?

"An excellent choice!" Betsy said as she whipped out a tape measure. "It almost fits you perfectly."

If it fit so perfectly, why was she measuring everything?

"So you can have a tailored dress on your wedding day," Kelly answered the question I hadn't asked. It was kind of spooky.

It took another hour just to get the measurements down. We walked over to the register, and she handed me the price tag.

"Wait! What?" I balked. "Three thousand dollars? Does it come with a limousine and open bar?"

"Ooooh! I forgot to order the limo!" Kelly smacked her forehead.

I continued to protest. "The dress! It's too expensive."

Kelly put her hands on her hips. "That's how much wedding dresses cost these days. Stop being such a big baby."

I reluctantly handed over my credit card and watched very carefully to make sure she didn't add any more zeros. Money wasn't really a problem. The principal of wearing a garment that expensive only once was.

Betsy handed the card back. "I'll call you in a month when it comes in, and we'll have a fitting. When's the wedding?"

"December fifteenth," Kelly replied.

"It's so far away…" I said. Maybe I didn't have to make this decision just yet.

"Oh, no, it isn't!" Betsy grinned. "If we need another fitting, this will give us some wiggle room."

Kelly gave the woman her number. Once we were outside, she explained she didn't have a lot of faith in me to come back.

I stopped and turned toward her. "I paid three grand for that dress. Why wouldn't I come back?"

"Let's get some lunch," Kelly said. "You'll feel better."

We were just walking into the Chinese restaurant on Main when Rex passed in his car. He pulled over, and we invited him to join us.

"Really?" he said as we were seated. "You bought the dress?" I was a little insulted that his voice had such a ring of shock to it.

Kelly nodded. "And it's perfect. Have you ordered your tux?"

"With top hat and tails?" I added.

He rolled his eyes. "So, you've been to see my sisters again?"

"They gave me this lovely stuffed blue jay to wear as a brooch." I left out the part where I'd destroyed the brooch by escaping a fire. "Randi said she was going to make one for your top hat."

Rex buried his face in his hands. "I was afraid of this. I suppose they told you about the various traditions, too?"

The waitress interrupted, so we ordered.

After she'd gone, I leaned forward. "Yeah, we're not doing any of those. Especially not the haggis thing."

"Come on," Kelly protested. "These are all Ferguson family traditions. You have to do them."

"Why don't we come up with our own?" I asked. "Maybe something with the cats?"

"How about," Rex interrupted, "we just keep things simple."

"If you have all of these traditions," Kelly said, "you should try to adopt one or two. In my family every bride is given a triple strand of pearls. That's not so bad."

"In my family," Rex said slowly, "the bride and groom have a sword fight."

"I am not having a swordfight in a three-thousand-dollar dress!" I shouted a little too loudly.

Diners on either side of us gave us the strangest looks.

"I'm very good at sword fighting," I said loudly.

Rex shook his head, and I wondered if he was up to the challenge. Would it be sabers or foils? How did you get blood out of satin?

I changed the subject. "What's up with all these fires lately?"

Rex relaxed. This was familiar territory. This was where he told me to stay out of it and I ignored him.

"You'll see it on the news tonight anyway. There have been three fires. Two non-residential, one residential."

"Really?" I lied. "Where was the residential one? The fire trucks sounded close yesterday."

Kelly kicked me under the table.

"It was just a couple of blocks away from us," Rex said. "The fire marshal thinks the fires at the arena last month and the ice cream shop the other day are related, but not the house fire."

I leaned forward. "What do you think?" Getting away with seeming surprised was making me bolder.

Rex took a long drink of his iced tea. "Personally? I think that…"

The waitress dropped off our stir-fry and walked away. I tackled the crab rangoons like it was the first time I'd eaten food.

To my complete surprise, Rex leaned forward. "I think they are all related. I don't know why, and I can't prove it. But something's up. A couple of my men think they've seen Feds around town." He leaned back again and gave me a look. "You haven't heard from Riley, have you?"

Suddenly, I wasn't hungry anymore. This was the part where I either lied to my future husband or told him the truth. Frankly, I didn't want to do either. Fortunately, my mouth was full of fried cream cheese and sweet and sour sauce.

Kelly jumped in. "It's arson?" She put her hand to her chest. "That's terrifying. Makes me want to check the batteries on the smoke alarms when I get home. Especially if the arsonist has moved to houses now."

Rex patted her arm. "I don't think you need to worry about that. In fact, I was concerned when the TV stations started calling this morning. I don't want to start a panic. That's the last thing we need."

We ate in silence for a moment.

I swallowed. "There's a quote by Ian Fleming that's appropriate. *Once is happenstance. Twice is coincidence. Three times is enemy action.* That kind of fits here, I think."

Rex's eyebrows went up. "You and I agree with the creator of James Bond. The fires are happening too close together. But I can see where it doesn't make sense."

"Who lived at the house that burned down?" I asked with the most innocent expression I could manage.

My fiancé sighed and pushed his Mongolian beef away. "That young woman who's gone missing. The one who worked for our veterinarian."

I was pretty sure I looked stunned. It was hard to tell without a mirror, and I feared that holding one up to check might be a giveaway.

"Kate?" I asked.

Rex nodded. "Kate Becks. Ever heard of her?"

Kelly and I looked at each other before shaking our heads.

I snapped my fingers. "I know that name." I made a big show of trying to think. "Your sisters were talking about someone named Kate who hasn't picked up her order." I turned to Kelly, "It's a cat on a Roomba."

Kelly sighed. "I've always wanted a Roomba."

"Did they?" Rex scowled. Maybe he didn't like the idea of his sisters being involved. Or maybe he was starting to suspect my involvement.

My mind raced. "You should check with my therapist, Susan…and see if Kate Becks is the client who blew her off."

Rex's right eyebrow went up. "You seem to know a lot about this missing woman, considering you said you don't know her."

I shrugged. "It's just coincidence that in the same twenty-four hours, my vet and your sisters all mentioned the same name."

Rex nodded. "Like you said. Three times is an enemy action." He got up. "I'll take care of the bill. I have to get back to work." He kissed me on the forehead. "And I'll talk to you later."

CHAPTER FIFTEEN

———

Kelly and I split up. We had a couple of hours before the Scout meeting started. I had to get some poster board and other supplies. Kelly had to pick up some books on France from the library.

As I ran my errands, I couldn't help but gloat a little. Rex now knew that Kate was the missing woman. I just needed to give him a little push so he'd make the connection between her and the Fontanas.

And I knew just how to do it.

"Hey neighbor!" I waved at Mark Fontana as I pulled a suitcase on wheels behind me. I always walked to the meetings, and I didn't have a wagon. Maybe I should get one?

Mark smiled tightly. "Merry! What's up?"

"I was thinking about what you said the other day. About dinner. How about it? You and Pam can meet Rex and me somewhere. Name the time and place!" A double date would lower their guard, and I could ask seemingly innocent questions, like *Have you ever been to Russia* or *Did you kidnap and kill Kate Becks*?

"Okay." He looked around as if concerned that we were on camera. "How about tomorrow night at The American?"

Oh brother. This guy was going over the top trying to prove he was who he wasn't. American food, apple pie, Yankee pot roast—it was embarrassing.

"Sounds great. Say seven?" I asked.

He nodded, and I continued on my way, texting the details to Rex as I walked. I wasn't good at that. A couple of times, I fell off the sidewalk. But it was all set. Just a cozy dinner between three spies and a cop. Totally normal.

"Girls!" I called out as I entered the classroom. "Ready to get some work done?"

A loud cheer went up as I handed out poster board and markers. Kelly distributed the books on France.

"We need to put together some ideas for a display," Kelly said. She pointed at a table full of Kaitlyns. "You ladies have to come up with food ideas. Something simple we can serve—nothing too complicated."

The table with Betty, Lauren, Ava, and Inez volunteered to look for a French game or folk dance they could teach the kids at Thinking Day. Caterina, the two Hannahs, and Emily decided they would find a craft project for the make-it take-it table.

Kelly and I circulated.

"Mrs. Wrath?" one of the Kaitlyns asked. "Can we make crepes?"

I shook my head. "I don't think we can take a griddle in there. Keep looking."

Great. Now I wanted crepes. Too bad the nearest French restaurant was in Omaha. That made me think of Riley. I shoved those thoughts from my head.

"We could do foie gras. Or crème brûlée," one of the girls added. The others seemed to agree. I was impressed. These girls had done their research.

"Like I said, we can't take an oven in, and we can't serve anything that needs a bowl or plate. It has to be finger food."

A collective gasp filled the air. "Fingers as food?" one of the girls cried out. "Are the French monsters?"

"No, *finger food* means…" But I was outmatched.

Betty slammed her fist on the table. "I knew it! I knew it!"

"*Finger food* means food you can eat *with* your fingers," I said.

"Why can't we just do french fries?" another Kaitlyn asked.

"With a nice burgundy," added another.

A third Kaitlyn shook her head. "There's no meat, so no red wine. I think a chardonnay might work though."

The others nodded as if this was perfectly normal, and I didn't say anything because the problem basically solved itself.

They wouldn't be able to bring wine into the Expo Center anyway. And if somehow they did, I'd confiscate it, which meant free wine for me.

"I think," Betty was saying, "that we should teach people the national anthem of France…'Le Marseillaise.'"

Uh-oh.

"What's it about?" Lauren asked.

"Girls," I interrupted, "maybe you should do 'Frère Jacque'?"

Inez was on her phone with Ava looking over her shoulder. "Here it is! Let's see… Ooooh! Listen to this! *The soldiers are coming into our arms to slit the throats of our sons and women! Let the impure blood soak into our fields!*"

Betty grumped, "Pretty threatening from a bunch of flag droppers."

"Okay!" I held up my hands. "You are not doing 'Le Marseillaise.' Find something else."

"But…" Ava complained.

I stood firm on this. "Nope! Not gonna happen."

Inez continued on as if she never heard me. "There's something about tigers tearing at women's boobies!"

This aroused the interest of the girls at the other tables.

"Nope," I said again. "Not doing that. Find something nice and sweet." I pointed at Betty and motioned for her to come to me.

"You can't blame me," Betty said quickly. "I didn't write the French national anthem. Although if I did, I'd probably come up with something like that."

No doubt. "This isn't about that. I just heard you're a decent hacker."

The girl looked around as if she might have spies surrounding her. "White hat or black hat?"

"It's classified. Can you help me with this?" I pulled the laptop out of my bag.

The little girl sat down at a separate table, away from the rest of the girls, and started typing.

"What are you doing?" Kelly appeared at my side.

"What? You suggested Betty as a hacker."

She frowned. "I didn't really think you'd go through with it."

Why wouldn't she think I'd go through with it?

Kelly continued, "I don't think I can let you do this. We have to protect the girls. What if there's something horrible on that laptop? Like pictures of murders?"

I was pretty confident that would be right up the girl's alley. "I think of this more like experience for her future."

Betty was, of all my girls, most likely to be a spy. Maybe it was my duty to make sure she did it for the right team. Hey! That sounded good. I was just about to tell my co-leader this, but she was pulled away by the "food" table.

"I'm in," Betty called out, and I sat down next to her.

I squinted at the screen. "Really? That didn't take long."

Betty gave me a look usually reserved for people far more grown up than me. "Don't underestimate me."

"Okay." I took the laptop back.

In a hushed voice, she said, "I set you up with a new password. That way you can get on it anytime. It's *poopyhead2*."

"Why not *poopyhead1*?"

Betty shrugged. "That's *my* password." She rolled her eyes. "And now, I'll have to change it."

And with that, she stomped off and rejoined her table and their discussion on French folk dances. That seemed like a safe bet. Safer than "Le Marseillaise."

"How's it going?" I asked Kelly.

"Not bad. The Kaitlyns have come up with serving mini éclairs—which I can get in bulk from the store. They wanted French roast coffee, but we're dealing with little kids, so they're still looking for something to drink. Did you realize how much they know about wine?"

I nodded. "Looks like Lauren's table"—I carefully avoided pointing out Betty and reminding her of what I'd just had the girl do—"has come up with a dance to teach. That's good."

Kelly nodded. "The other table is struggling with a make-it take-it craft. Any thoughts?"

I walked over. The girls were making sketches.

"Any ideas?" I asked, a little afraid of the answer.

Caterina looked up. "Either pipe cleaner Eiffel tower pins, or little French flag pins."

"For SWAPS," Emily added.

SWAPS stands for *Special Whatchamacallits Affectionately Pinned Somewhere* and, as you can guess from the name, are little pins that Girl Scouts make to trade with each other. In the past I've had to vote down SWAPS made to resemble Bowie knives, submachine guns, and one creative blood-soaked hatchet.

"Flags sound easy." And much better.

We ended the meeting with a shopping list of things for Kelly and me to get—construction paper, pins, glue, tablecloths, etc. The girls went home with a note telling their parents that they needed black pants and shoes.

"How much time before Thinking Day?" I asked as we packed up.

"Another week. I'd say we're ahead of the game." Kelly waved and headed to her car.

I shoved the laptop into my rolling bag and headed home. As I passed by the Fontanas' place I re-texted Rex about dinner the next night. He texted back that he was busy with his various investigations but that we should go so I wouldn't snoop anymore.

Sitting at the breakfast bar minutes later, I poured a healthy glass of wine and opened up the laptop. After typing in my new password, the screen came up with a couple dozen file folders, all named with numbers. This would take a while.

The little twinges of guilt I felt for keeping this from Rex faded as I clicked on the first folder. Cat pictures flooded the screen. Mr. Pickles, Kate's deceased and Roomba-affixed pet, appeared in all of them. Orange tabby cats usually looked angry, and this cat was no exception.

I continued opening files and got photo after photo of the deceased Mr. Pickles. There were pictures of him eating (and looking angry), eating angry, staring out the window angry, and a couple with his angry face sticking out of the top of his cat box. I understood that one.

The last folder was devoted to the cat in various costumes. This was at least interesting. Mr. Pickles dressed as

Santa, Satan, the Easter Bunny, and, in one bizarre moment of humiliation, as a dog. I tried to picture Philby letting me do this. I made a mental note to have a tiny version of my wedding dress made—just for her.

I spent the rest of the night searching Kate Becks' laptop, without success. There wasn't anything that even remotely implied she was a spy. No lists of incriminating people or activities, no spreadsheets indicating she was getting mysterious payments from a bank in the Caymans, no *aha* moments whatsoever.

Even her internet history was limited to Amazon purchases (cat toys and books about cats), Google searches for pictures of cats, YouTube funny cat videos, and a site about linguine that didn't seem to fit at all.

I closed the computer at eleven p.m. and sat there, thinking. According to this, Kate Becks was clean. So, why hide it in a secret room with a dummy and a jar of lemon juice?

People can be weird. Maybe she had a safe room, just for fun. Maybe she fantasized about being a secret agent (or a cat). Had I gotten it all wrong?

Face it, Wrath, you've been out of the game for two years. Like Susan said, I was prematurely expelled from a great career, and I missed it. Was I just imagining these things because I wanted them to be true?

Now, Kate was missing. It might just be that she snapped and ran off. Maybe she took a vacation without telling her boss, her therapist, and her taxidermist.

Once is happenstance. Twice is coincidence. Three times is enemy action.

Ian Fleming's words kept running through my brain. It was possible I was projecting onto this series of events—the fires, the body the Fontanas carried, the missing woman—and was trying to make something out of nothing.

Or…there *was* something and my spy-dy sense was right all along. Dinner with the Fontanas might be just what I needed to prove my case.

"Tomorrow," I said to Philby, "I'm going out to dinner with the neighbors. If they're spies—I'll know it."

Philby belched, before turning and walking away. Apparently, she was unimpressed.

CHAPTER SIXTEEN

———

"You look great!" Rex greeted me with a kiss as he picked me up for dinner.

"You too," I said.

Rex was dashing as ever, in a black silk shirt and khaki slacks. He was a striking man with the athletic build of a Roman God. I was never one of those women who went gaga over big muscles. Rex's physique was lean and muscular. And he didn't flaunt it. Which was good because he was all mine.

If she were alive, Grandma Wrath would've said Rex had a nice fanny—referring to his nice, shapely butt. Old Iowans were either *keister* people or *fanny* people and used those two terms liberally. But, you couldn't be both a *fanny* and a *keister* person. The rules regarding rustic terminology are pretty strict on that.

It wasn't until I started field work as a spy that I learned that one of those terms had a different meaning abroad. In the UK, *fanny* inexplicably means lady parts. The *front* parts. I learned that lesson the hard way at a gala at the British Embassy in Colombia. To be fair, I'd had four martinis when I kind of shouted that Riley shouldn't slap the ambassador's wife on the fanny.

Security had quickly escorted us from the building. I've heard from colleagues that our pictures are still posted at the front desk, with *Deny Entry* in large red letters across the top. We'd even heard rumors that the guards are allowed to shoot us on sight, but that's probably not true.

I was wearing a little black dress and ballet flats. I'd even managed to tame my hair into a semblance of a shape. Granted, it was the shape of an epileptic octopus in mid-seizure, but it was a shape nonetheless.

He kissed me again, and my heart fluttered. I really did love him. So why was I freaking out? I knew it didn't make much sense, but that was hardly comforting.

The American was a nice restaurant with a northwestern theme featuring elk and bears. A giant stuffed moose confronted us in the entryway. I wondered if Randi and Ronni had done it.

"Over here!" Mark waved from a table in the dining room.

We joined the couple, and I was introduced to Pam. Both of them looked like they belonged here. But while Mark was fifty shades of normal, Pam had a sharp eye, always examining things, paying rapt attention as if she'd need this information later.

In a way, it felt validating.

Rex ordered the wine and the sommelier delivered it. I watched as my future husband had the first taste and approved of the choice, and then the waiter poured for all of us. Rex was so amazing. What did he see in me?

"How about a toast?" Mark asked. Holding his glass in the air he said, "To neighbors! There's nothing more American than that!"

What a strange thing to say. Definitely suspicious.

When the waiter left, we fell into some idle chatter about nothing. Pam asked about the school at the end of the block and seemed interested that I was a Scout leader.

"Did you choose the house because of the school?" I asked. I thought it might be rude to ask if they planned to have kids.

Many illegals did. It helped them fit in and made them look like they belonged. But if I had to guess, these two were in their late thirties, so kids might not be in the cards for them.

Pam cocked her head to one side, kind of like an inquisitive pug. "No. When we bought the house, it hadn't occurred to us that there was a school."

How could they not notice a huge elementary school on the other end of the block?

Mark laughed. "Imagine our surprise when, at 2:40, the sidewalk was flooded with kids."

Pam studied Rex. "Is that why you moved to your house? Because you wanted to start a family?" She glanced at me with a smirk in her eyes.

My stomach clenched. I hadn't thought of that. Did he want kids? I didn't. I already had twelve of them, and they were a handful.

Rex grinned. "No. I just liked the house and the neighborhood." He reached over and held my hand. "I'm not ruling them out though."

For a second it felt like ice ran in my veins. We hadn't discussed this until this very moment. You'd think a couple would discuss that before marriage, right?

"Of course," my fiancé added, "that's something we will have to discuss at some point."

My neck started sweating. What the heck? Whose neck sweats when they're nervous?

"Merry," Pam said with a smile I couldn't interpret, "you must love kids, since you're working with them."

Was it getting hot in here? I wasn't even thirty, and I was perspiring like a middle-aged menopausal woman on the equator.

"I do," I said slowly. "And I have a lovely little goddaughter, but for now, this is all I can handle."

"That's right," Mark said. "You don't have a day job, do you?"

Pam stared at me. "I wish I didn't have a day job."

Mark slipped his arm around his wife. "It's better, though, because we are our own bosses. Right hon?"

Pam smiled at him. "Yes. That's true. Still"—she indicated me with her wine glass—"I'd love to lie around the house all day."

Is that what people thought I did? Nothing? That seemed unfair. But come to think of it, the only other women I knew who stayed at home were married and had kids. Well, except for this author I knew of who lived down the street. But as far as I knew, she wasn't right in the head.

Rex squeezed my hand. "Merry's still figuring out what she wants to do."

Okay, I got that he was helping me, but what did that mean? He knew I was a spy before. But how did he really feel about the fact that I didn't work now? One more thing in our to-be-discussed pile.

"I'm hoping she'll find her niche," he said with a smile. "Figure out what she wants to do."

Since when did I have to find something to do? And why were my ear lobes sweating now? I was turning into a mess. I was supposed to be reading these people, and instead, I was getting carried away with my insecurity. I had an appointment with Susan for the next day. I'd have to bring this up to her. Yes. That was it. *Save it for later, Wrath.*

I shook everything off and smiled as warmly as I could.

"I think it's marvelous, you two working together in your own business. If I joined the police force, I think Rex would have second thoughts."

My fiancé laughed. Loudly. "Merry sometimes has opinions about my job."

Everybody laughed, and I kicked him under the table. Opinions? I'd helped him solve some very complicated cases over the time I'd known him. Maybe he wouldn't want people knowing that.

"I wish I was a detective," I said. "I think I'd enjoy it."

"I'm sure it's pretty quiet," Pam said. "It's such a small town—not much happens around here."

Mark disagreed. "That's not true. There have been some fires here in the last week or so. I thought I saw that on the news. Isn't that right, Rex?"

The Fontanas looked eagerly at Rex. Either they were very curious, or they wanted intel on what was going on, which would be a huge benefit to their operation if they were spies. Did they just befriend Rex to pump him for information?

My fiancé had a wonderful talent for telling people what he knew and making it sound like super-secret intel, when all it really was, was a rehash of the public news.

He nodded. "That's right. Three fires—all arson. The fire marshal thinks it must be kids. But we'll catch them."

Kids? Now that was a cover if I ever heard one. He didn't really think it was kids, did he? I realized I hadn't really seen him much lately. He was so busy with work, and I was busy with being a lunatic (a full-time occupation lately).

Dinner arrived, which stopped all conversation. All four of us had steak. As we cut into the juicy, Iowa grass-fed beef, an awkward silence settled around us. This had been harder than I'd thought. Sure, they were acting strange, but as I ran through the conversation in my head, there wasn't any one clue that stood out. If I was going to catch these guys in something, I was running out of time.

"Tell Pam about your cats," Mark said, pointing to his wife with his knife as if I wasn't sure I knew who he was talking about.

"I have two cats," I said as I wiped my mouth on my napkin. "One looks like Hitler, the other like Elvis."

Mark nodded. "They really do. I've seen them in your window, staring at me. It's pretty weird."

"The larger one is named Philby." I watched their faces carefully. Philby was named after a famous Englishman who spied for the Russians.

Their expressions were unreadable. Actually, they were trying hard to look blank.

"And Martini," Rex said. "She had two other kittens, but Dr. Body has them."

"Dr. Body?" Pam's eyebrows went up.

"She's the coroner for the county," I said. "She's very *thorough*." I put all my emphasis on the last word in hopes of tripping them up. "You can't put anything past her."

"How interesting," Pam said. "Don't you think that's interesting, Mark?"

They exchanged a strange glance I couldn't interpret.

"You know," Mark said, "now that you mention it, there have been an unusual number of murders for a town this size."

Hmmm...

Rex nodded. "You're right. It does keep my department busy."

The four of us continued eating in silence. One, because the conversation was heading in a strange direction, and two, because our mouths were full of yummy, yummy steak. And you should never talk with your mouth full of yummy, yummy steak.

As I ate, I realized I'd been played. The beginning of our conversation was meant to throw me off, make me uncomfortable, distract me. And it did. Oh, these two were good. I'd have to fix that.

The empty plates were carried off, and a dessert menu was handed to Rex, who the waiter had deemed the leader of this little group.

"So, Mark," I said, "why did you guys move here?"

Mark frowned for just a moment. I'd caught him off guard. But in seconds he was smiling again. "I thought I told you. We bought the business from a couple who wanted to retire."

Pam spoke up quickly, almost interrupting him. "It just made sense, right, Mark? We wanted a quiet life in the country. And this is close enough to Des Moines to make it seem less isolated."

"Did you take on all of the clients the original owners left behind?" I asked. "Or have you had to find new clients?"

"We inherited the folks we have," Mark answered.

Pam said, "We really are quite busy."

Rex's cell buzzed, and he looked at it. "I'm sorry. I have to step outside and take this. I'll be right back."

As soon as he walked away, I started on a new tack.

"I think some of my friends are clients of yours. Robert and Kelly Albers?" I watched their faces. "And Kate Becks?"

I didn't take my eyes off them, but I noticed the slightest reaction. Pam seemed to be sweating, and a vein throbbed in Mark's neck.

"We can't disclose information about our clients, I'm afraid." Pam smiled, but her demeanor had changed just a tiny bit, from challenging to hostile.

I waved them off. "Oh sure. I totally understand. Not sure what I was thinking."

Mark relaxed a bit. "We sure like it here, but with a small town, you have lots of people who know your business."

I looked directly at him. "No secrets in this place. Everyone knows what their neighbors are up to."

The atmosphere was practically crackling with tension.

Pam cleared her throat, a terse smile on her face. "That's so true. In fact, we've noticed you're up pretty late at night."

"That's funny." I lifted my wine glass. "I've noticed the same thing about you."

No one spoke. We were engaged in a spy stare-down. I hoped I was winning.

Mark broke the silence with nervous laughter. "Well, we've always been night owls. The business keeps us busy, and sometimes we work late into the night."

On insurance claims, or espionage? My lie-dar went into overdrive.

"Why are you up at night, Merry?" Pam asked pointedly.

"Me? Oh, I have insomnia. Lately all this wedding planning is stressing me out. I had no idea how many things the bride is responsible for."

Pam relaxed a bit. "That makes sense."

Rex joined us. "I'm afraid there's been an incident I need to look after. I apologize, but we must be going." He pulled out my chair for me.

"I'll get the bill." Mark waved us off.

Rex shook his hand. "I already paid it. You can get it next time."

We said our goodbyes and made our way to Rex's car.

"What's going on? Is it another fire? The missing woman?" I was vibrating with anticipation. Or maybe it was the coffee.

My fiancé opened my door for me. "No. I just figured I'd get you out of there before Pam stabbed you with a fork."

I nodded as he got in on his side. "She was rather tense, wasn't she?"

Rex turned to me. "Probably from the third degree you gave her."

"I was just being friendly." I pouted.

"Listen, Merry, I know you suspect them of…whatever you saw the other night. But people are innocent until proven guilty. If there's something wrong with them, I'll investigate it."

Should I tell him about my suspicions? How could I do that without implicating myself? Rex had no idea about my break-in at Kate Becks' house. He hated it when I meddled. Something in the back of my mind told me to play nice.

"Got it."

He pulled into my driveway and leaned over and kissed me. All the tension of the evening kind of faded away. He really was an excellent kisser.

"Just try to get some sleep for once," he said. "Okay?"

I nodded and got out of the car. Rex waited in the driveway until I was inside my house before pulling into his own driveway across the street.

I decided to keep any further theories to myself until it was time to show him I was right. And I had an idea where to start next.

CHAPTER SEVENTEEN

———

"What, exactly, is wrong with Philby?" Dr. Alvarez stared at the cat, who in turn looked at me as if to ask the same question.

"She's not eating," I lied.

That might not have been the right excuse, as the vet poked and prodded my obese pet. To be fair, I hadn't slept much the night before. I know, I sound like a broken record. And this broken record wasn't thinking straight if she just told the vet her cat was starving.

"Really? She looks like she's been doubling up on the meals lately."

The previous night I'd decided that in order to find out more about Kate Becks, I needed to do my own investigating. And what seemed like a brilliant idea kind of dimmed in the morning light as I realized it looked like I was guilty of Munchausen by proxy.

"Oh! Sorry!" I smacked my forehead for good measure. "I mean, she's eating too much. Sorry about that."

Dr. Alvarez smiled. "I understand that. Since we're shorthanded around here, even the vets are washing cages and closing up shop each night." She stifled a yawn.

What a perfect opportunity! "Right, I forgot you said you had a staff member who hasn't shown up for work. Did my fiancé call you about that?"

The vet yawned again. "He did. Thank you for that. I honestly don't know which end is up. I can't even remember what Kate did around here, but it must have been a lot, because we're swamped."

"Kate…" I tapped my chin. "Do you mean Kate Becks?"

Dr. A looked down over the top of her glasses at me. "Yes. That's right. How did you know?"

"She's an acquaintance. A friend of a friend, you could say. I know lots of people who've said she just up and vanished."

The vet nodded. "That's right. That's exactly it."

"So, she did a good job here? That's why you're so busy?"

There was the briefest hesitation. "She did. She would've loved Philby. She was crazy for cats."

That part I already knew.

"How long did she work here?" I tried to keep the conversation casual so as not to raise suspicion.

"Not long. Maybe six months? I'm not sure. My business manager, Sally, she would know." Dr. Alvarez was so tired, she didn't notice my questioning.

She took Philby away to weigh her, and I sat there in the exam room, thinking. I hadn't really learned that much about Kate here. Except that she hasn't been here long. I'd need a little more to go on. I could pump the receptionist on my way out.

Dr. Alvarez returned. "Philby is seriously overweight. Like the size of three cats combined."

Philby looked annoyed. But then, she always looked like that.

The vet handed me some samples. "You need to start feeding her this. The way she looks, I'd almost say you're giving her tuna every day. But that would be ridiculous, right?"

"Right!" I did give her tuna every day. "Who would do something like that?"

Dr. A frowned. "You'd be surprised, really."

She told me to make an appointment in a month to check on Philby's progress. I headed out to the receptionist. The kid behind the counter must've been no older than twenty. The nameplate said *MacKenzee.*

"Doc wants to see you again in a month." She rolled her eyes and cracked her gum loudly. "*Now* I gotta turn on the computer."

"That's right. I'm free most of the time, so just about any day will work."

This kid should be easy to pump intel out of.

"Whatever," MacKenzee said.

I adjusted Philby under my arm. She was too big for the cat carrier. "Have I seen you here before, or are you new?"

MacKenzee shrugged. "Depends on how you define new. Mom works here. They said some airhead ran off and they needed help."

"You didn't know the woman who disappeared, then?"

The computer screen came on, and the girl sighed like a martyr. "No, but from what I've heard, she sounds like a total loser."

"What have you heard?" I leaned forward conspiratorially.

MacKenzee poked a few buttons on the keyboard before scowling at the screen. "She's a weirdo, she's obsessed with cats, had no friends, and wasn't friendly here. Mom called her paranoid."

Paranoid—that's what I was looking for.

"Oh?" Sometimes one-syllable words are all you need.

"Yeah. Like she was always looking over her shoulder. People suck. That's what I was telling Bob."

Philby hissed so hard she shot backwards out of my arms onto the counter. She just lay there, legs wiggling, like an obese jellybean.

"I'm sorry. That name's a trigger for her. Bad memories from a former owner." I righted my cat.

"What? You mean Bob?" MacKenzee said again.

Philby hissed loudly, rolling onto her back and kicking like a fat tick in an attempt to get up.

"Man!" the girl said. "Neat trick." For a brief sliver of a second, the kid almost smiled. Almost.

I lifted my cat back onto her feet. "Please don't say it again."

MacKenzee sighed heavily and rolled her eyes. I'd taken her fun away.

She turned her attention to the computer monitor and frowned. "Looks like I can fit you in any day. *What* do you *want?*" She made the question sound like I was making an outrageous demand.

We picked a time and date, and the teenager handed me an appointment card. I ran out the door, hoping to make it out before we had another episode.

As we drove home, I thought about what she'd said. No friends, always paranoid, obsessed with her cat… Kate Becks sounded like a spy to me. Albeit, a bad one. The idea was to blend in, not stand out. And she stood out enough to get noticed.

I had to find a photo of her. All I'd found in her house and on her computer were pictures of Mr. Pickles. That seemed like a rookie spy move too. Everybody has family pictures or something like that in their house. I had a picture of my parents on my nightstand, and a photo of Rex and me at a Girl Scout carnival fundraiser. I also have a huge portrait of Kelly and me with our troop after wallowing in a mud pit.

See? I lived alone and kind of off the grid, and I had lots of mementos.

Kate Becks, had none.

Kate Becks had to be a spy. And for some reason, Mark and Pam Fontana were involved. I just couldn't get over how many spies were in Who's There. This had to be some sort of record. Was there a place in the Guinness Book of World Records for how many international spooks you could fit into a small town?

Of course, Rex didn't think there were any spies here…other than me. And I fit more into the former-spy category. Would Riley know about the Fontanas? He was a spy. He could probably spot one a mile away.

Next time I saw him, I was going to tie him to a chair and make him talk. Did I still have that blowtorch and tongs? I'd have to look because I hadn't seen them in a while. Oh well. An ordinary toothpick would work instead. You wouldn't believe the intel I've uncovered using just one toothpick.

I dropped Philby off at home, where she went right to her food dish. When I poured the new diet dry food onto her plate, she looked at me, then the plate, then me, then the plate. Instead of explaining it to her, I raced out the door to my appointment with Susan.

I'd been able to get in a little early. Getting information from her would be much harder, since she had patient confidentiality and all that. Somehow, I'd have to get information without seeming to get it at all.

"Merry!" Susan greeted me warmly and motioned to a chair.

I sat. "Thanks for seeing me. I just felt like we made some progress last time. I needed to talk about this more."

The counselor waved me off. "Not a problem. My workload is a little lighter right now."

Nice segue! Maybe it was Be Nice to a Former Spy Day!

"Oh!" I exclaimed. "Because of that patient who disappeared. I'd forgotten!"

Susan nodded and cut right to the chase. "What should we talk about today?"

I was prepared for this. "My career as a spy." I studied her reaction.

If she was surprised, she didn't show it. Either she was that good or she'd heard something like this before. From Kate Becks.

"You were a spy?" she asked. There wasn't a shred of teasing in those words. She'd meant them.

I nodded. "I worked for the CIA. I had a partner, and we worked together in situations all over the world."

Susan nodded. "You liked your job?"

"I did." I explained how I'd had to retire early because I'd been outed by the vice president of the USA as a stab at my father—a prominent member of the Senate.

Susan's eyebrows went up at that. Which told me she didn't believe me. "I don't think we have a senator named Wrath," she said.

"My dad's name isn't Wrath. It's Czrygy. Senator Czrygy."

"Really? I love your dad!" Susan was excited. "His work on passing the mental health bill through Congress was amazing."

He did that? I needed to show more interest in my father's work.

The therapist settled back against her seat, scribbling something in a notebook. And that's when it hit me. She kept written records. Files of her interviews with clients. And since I liked Susan and wanted to keep seeing her, this was a way I could find out more without bugging her. I just needed to get hold of Kate Becks' file.

How was I going to do that?

"Let's talk about the outing," Susan said. "How did that make you feel?"

A mosh pit of emotions slam danced in my head. No one had ever asked me that before. Strange.

"I hated leaving the agency," I said slowly. "I loved my job. It was interesting. Fun. Dangerous. I thought I'd be there until retirement." All of that was true.

Susan nodded. "It must have been a huge shock. A major life change."

I nodded vigorously. "Yes! It was! I got to see the world, go places, meet people. Now, I'm back in the small town I'd wanted to escape."

Wait! Did I really feel that way?

"Do you resent it?"

I thought about this. "No. Yes. Maybe? I mean, I resented the vice president, obviously. And I resented the agency. Even though there wasn't much they could do. Well, that's not totally true. I could've worked a desk job. I just wanted to make a clean break, I guess."

Susan wrote something down. "Do you resent your father?"

"What?" That came out of left field. "No. It wasn't his fault."

"What about your fiancé?"

I frowned. "No, I don't resent him. Why would I resent him?"

She shrugged. "I'm not saying you do. It would be normal to do so, however. Rex is a detective. You used to be a kind of detective. He gets to keep doing his job, but you don't get to keep doing yours."

It seemed as if the oxygen went out of the room. I shoved one thought from my mind and seized upon the other.

"Do you think that's it? Is that why I'm so nervous about the wedding?" If so, it didn't seem very nice of me. Rex couldn't help it that his job was something I wanted. Was I holding that against him?

Susan cocked her head to one side. "I don't know. My job is to help you explore all options. Sometimes things look one way, but underneath they turn out to be very different. While this might not be the main reason for your insomnia, it might be one piece of the puzzle."

I sat back, letting this wash over me. There was some truth in what she was saying.

"What do I do with this information?" I asked after a lengthy pause.

"That's up to you. The most important thing about it is how it affects your outlook on Rex, on the wedding, and anything else." She sat back.

I bit my lip. "Wow. That's pretty impressive. You know, I've talked to my parents, my fiancé, my best friend, and a few animals, and they never offered me this level of insight."

Susan smiled. "Don't overthink it. This might be part of the problem, or it might not. We've got a lot more work to do."

I shook my head. "I can't believe I didn't think of that."

"It was always in your head. It just needed to be coaxed out."

I jumped to my feet and shook her hand. "Thank you! This is a huge breakthrough!"

"Wait," Susan said. "You still have time on the clock."

"I've got to go. I'll call to make another appointment." And with that, I was out the door.

I walked quickly to the nurse's station on the first floor. Kelly was standing at a counter with a clipboard. When she saw me, she seemed surprised.

"Merry! What are you doing here?"

"I won't bother you. I know you're working." I looked around carefully. "I just have one question. Did you tell Susan anything about me?"

Kelly thought for a moment. "Not really. Just that you are my best friend and that you are having wedding jitters."

"Did you tell her anything about Rex?"

"Rex?" Kelly looked off into the distance. "No. I'm pretty sure I didn't say anything more specific than the word fiancé. Why?"

I started off down the corridor, "I'll call you later! Bye!"

As I got into my car and turned the ignition, I realized I had another problem. One that never would have occurred to me.

Susan.

I never told her my fiancé's name or occupation.

So, how did she know his name was Rex and that he was a detective?

CHAPTER EIGHTEEN

———

Back at my house I started pacing back and forth. I'd been so sure I had this all figured out. The Fontanas were illegals—unreported foreign spies. Kate was too. Mark and Pam kidnapped and/or killed Kate. Easy. Cut and dry.

But now there was another player. Susan. And unless she was a private investigator too, she wouldn't know half of the things she'd just said to me. This was beyond complicated. Or I was paranoid. Did I mention it to the therapist? If only I could go back in time to find out what I'd said.

"What are you doing?" Riley's voice made me jump.

I spun around to see him, in a suit, smiling. "What are you doing here?"

"The door wasn't locked," he said. "You of all people should know the value of locked doors."

I'd have to work on that.

I glared, but maybe this was an opportunity. "Why do you keep stopping by?"

"Like I said, I'm just passing through…"

"…between Chicago and Omaha. Yeah. You've said that before. But I'm not buying it."

Riley sat down on the sofa. "Why don't you tell me what you think I'm doing here."

"I think you're here because of the Fontanas. The illegals next door."

Riley gave me a strange look. "I think you might be imagining things. Are you getting enough sleep?"

Fury rose inside me. If one more person tried to tell me I was imagining things, I was going to kill someone. Probably starting with Riley. No, definitely starting with Riley.

"I'm not imagining things. I'm completely serious. Something isn't right next door. And I think it's related to the missing woman." I pointed at him. "And you know that."

He frowned, lines marring his perfect features. "What missing woman?"

"Kate Becks. She works at my vet clinic and hasn't been seen for days."

Riley froze. "Did you say Kate Becks?"

Aha!

"You know her! I'm right!" I started doing a little end zone dance around the coffee table. Philby and Martini showed up and gave me one long look before scaling Riley and piling on top of each other in his lap.

Riley was staring into space. In fact, I was pretty sure he had no idea the cats were even on him. Oh yeah. He knew the missing woman, and he'd gone too far to deny it.

"Who is she?" I pressed.

"I can't tell you that." His lips formed a tight, grim line.

"Why not? We've worked together many times since I've moved here. You never kept things from me before."

Okay, that wasn't entirely true. In fact, he'd hidden lots from me over the last two years.

"Wrath, I…" His voice trailed off. "This is different."

"How is this different? I was a spy. Kate Becks is a spy. The Fontanas are spies. You used to be a spy."

He shook his head. "I'm not with the Agency anymore. I'm with the FBI."

I folded my arms over my chest. "So?"

"So, you have never been a Fed. I can't bring you on to a current investigation."

I looked around the room for something to throw at him. That's when I noticed he was dressed normally.

"You're not in disguise like you were the other times you stopped by."

"Nothing gets past you." He grinned.

My eyes narrowed. "Explain."

"No."

"Explain or I'll get some rope and mayonnaise and a Phillips-head screwdriver."

Riley gently nudged the cats off his lap. "I've got to go. I will tell you this: the name Kate Becks does ring a bell."

He stood over me, his eyes searching mine for something. I could swear his pheromones were in overdrive. Was he trying to seduce me? I took a step backward to dodge any advance.

"You should go." I walked over and held the door open for him.

Riley reached up and, very gently, stroked my cheek. I could feel my skin redden.

"Always good to see you, Merry." He kissed me on the forehead and left.

I shook off my confusion. This wasn't the right time to deal with whatever this was. Instead, I pulled up Kate's laptop and started going through it. Now that Riley confirmed that this woman was something, maybe I'd find something I'd missed before.

The woman was seriously obsessed with her dead cat. I looked over at my two felines. Philby was watching Martini chase her tail until she got dizzy and fell over. I guess I could understand Kate's love for her pets. Maybe I was even crazy enough to have them stuffed when they died. *Did I just think that?*

Picture after picture of Mr. Pickles sitting, eating, sleeping, and looking annoyed filled the screen. This was all Kate had on her laptop. It didn't make sense. If it's all just cat pictures, why was this in her safe room?

I took a break for lunch—which consisted of the easiest things to make in my house, a can of SpaghettiOs and package of leftover Scout cookies. Something was off. Was it her extreme focus on her cat? An idea crawled into my head, and I grabbed the keys and hit the road.

"Merry!" Randi clapped her hands with glee when I walked into Ferguson Taxidermy. "I'm so glad you're here! I had an idea for the wedding! It isn't ready yet, since the glue on the bull horns isn't completely dry, and..."

Ronni stomped into the room, preceded by her scowl. "You find that deadbeat who left the cat here?"

"Not yet." I smiled as affectionately as I could. "But I was wondering if I could look at her cat/Roomba thingy?"

"*No*." Ronni frowned, folding her arms over her chest.

"Now Ronni," Randi chastised. "Merry is trying to track this woman down for us. I can't see any harm in letting her see it."

The angry twin threw her hands up in the air. "I want no part of this!" And she left the room, muttering something about HIPPA laws and regulations.

"Don't worry." Randi smiled. "HIPPA only applies to people. Not their dead pets."

She led me to another room and pointed me toward the cat. The shotgun doorbell went off in the main showroom, and she excused herself.

As I approached the dead thing on the appliance, I couldn't help but admire the job they'd done. The feline cruiser looked like at any moment she'd hiss at me. The eyes seemed to take me in as I picked it up.

Of course, that meant I picked up the robot vacuum too. Which made it heavier. After a quick glance over my shoulder to make sure Randi wasn't there, I examined the small, round appliance.

Poking and prodding, I checked out every millimeter of the thing. I found the charging port and the dustbin. If Kate hid something, she wouldn't put it in the cat. The taxidermy twins would've found it. Besides, how would she put it in the cat? Wouldn't it come out the other end? My mind was taking me to a dark place I did not want to go.

No, she'd put it in the Roomba. I was sure of it. I continued to press buttons until the gadget came to life. I nearly dropped it, instead, setting it on the floor. The vacuum began to spin before it moved erratically across the floor.

The dead cat didn't seem to mind.

Why wasn't it moving in a straight line? That's how most folks vacuumed. But this was different. It almost looked like it was…I don't know, trying to tell me something as it curled to the right and left on its way across the floor.

"Oh!" Randi squeaked.

I scooped up the amalgamation of animal and appliance. "I'm sorry. It just went off."

"Did it?" Randi frowned as she took the deceased pet from me. "It hasn't been charged. Maybe it has a battery backup?"

My future sister-in-law found a tiny trapdoor I'd missed. I watched as she pressed it and it sprang open.

"A nine-volt?" Randi frowned. "How did I miss it?" She shrugged at me. "Normally we remove all power supplies when we work on something like this."

I stared at her, but why I was surprised after the blue jay, I'll never know. "You've done something like this before?"

She nodded. "We had an Irish client who had a badger he wanted holding a stun gun. Anyway, the thing went off on Ronni when she was attaching the animal to the device and zapped her. Dropped to the floor like a sack of potatoes. She wasn't right for two weeks after that."

Ronni had a "right"?

I peered into the tiny panel and extracted the battery. "What's this?" A small piece of paper was folded up under where the battery had been. I pulled it out.

"Was this your vacuum, or Kate's?" I asked.

"It was Kate's. We don't supply things like this anymore. Not since we put a moose on a Segway. The thing shorted and tore through our old shop like a bull in a china shop."

Or a moose on a Segway in any kind of shop.

The gunshot went off again, and Randi excused herself. That was good. I didn't want to read this in front of her. Very carefully, I unfolded the paper to find a phone number. It was the local area code and prefix. I didn't recognize the last four digits.

I refolded the note and stuffed it into my back pocket just as Randi appeared.

"What was it?" she asked.

"Just the warranty." I waved her off.

"Oh. Okay. I'm afraid I can't show you what I'm working on for the wedding. I have a new customer in the other room." Randi looked so sorrowful that I didn't tell her I was a smidge disappointed to find out what about my wedding required bull horns.

"That's fine. I can come back another time."

Upon entering the other room, I stopped dead in my tracks.

"Dr. Alvarez!" I may have said a little too loudly.

The veterinarian gave me a weak grin. "Ms. Wrath." She stood there, waiting for something. I was pretty sure she wanted me to leave. So, I did.

As I drove away I realized it wasn't that strange to see a vet at a taxidermist. In fact, I'd be willing to bet that people wanted their pets preserved more often than I'd want to think.

I wanted to go home and call the number on the note in my pocket. But a quick glance at the dashboard told me I had a more important meeting with my troop. I made it to the school just in time.

Kelly was in full-on leader mode as the girls worked on a mural featuring French icons. A plate of éclairs sat on a table, and I made a beeline for it.

Kelly shook her head. "One. You can have one. You're just as bad as the girls."

I took one éclair. I could've smuggled a second, but there were hard and fast rules about these kinds of things. Only taking one probably meant there was one for each girl only. I did a quick head count. Everyone was present and accounted for.

"Mrs. Wrath?" Betty tugged on my sleeve. "Did you find what you were looking for on that laptop?"

I drew her off to one side. "Not really. Just a bunch of pictures of a dead cat."

The girl's eyebrows went up. "A dead cat?"

"It was her pet. She had it stuffed."

"Maybe it's some sort of code?" Betty said before running back over to the painting in progress.

A code? How could dozens of pictures of an annoyed cat be a code? I had to admire Betty's imagination. I tried to think if the cat was forming a letter of the alphabet in any of the photos.

"Did you get the berets yet?" Kelly interrupted.

"They should be here in the next day or two," I said with a little pride in my voice.

"Good. Everything is almost ready. I'm starting to panic." She looked around the room.

"You?" I gasped. "Panic?"

Kelly couldn't panic! She was the calm one! What was I going to do if she panicked?

My co-leader closed her eyes and took a deep breath. She let it out and opened her eyes. "That's better. Ignore me."

"Why are you freaking out?"

"I had trouble finding the pink T-shirts, and I'm not sure how we're going to keep the éclairs cold. But it's nothing." She closed her eyes for a second. "Sorry. It's all right."

"Okay." I shrugged.

She turned to walk over to the plate of éclairs, which were now in the hands of the two Hannahs. "Don't forget, you have that sleep study tonight. At the hospital at ten."

Huh? "What are you talking about?"

Kelly rolled her eyes. "The sleep study! I signed you up for it. Remember?"

It dawned on me. "Oh. Right. Does it have to be tonight?"

"It's the only opening they have until next fall." Kelly shook her head. "I had to promise you'll be there."

I held up my hands. "No problem. I'll go tonight. What do I take?"

"Nothing. Just wear your pajamas." Kelly told me what room to report to. I told her I'd remember. She looked dubious.

For a moment, I thought about asking her to cancel. Spies and sleep studies don't usually mix well. In fact, you had to have another agent with you when you went under anesthesia. This would be a problem...if I was still a spy. But I wasn't. Not anymore. Granted, I'd worked on some cases that were still classified, but what the agency didn't know wouldn't hurt them. Right?

The girls called us over at that moment to look at the mural. Something nagged at me. I was on the verge of discovering something...but what was it?

The mural was actually quite nice. There was the Eiffel Tower, the Louvre, cheese, a couple of bottles of wine, and a herd of basset hounds. Susan, being the owner of bassets, would've liked that.

"What is this?" Kelly pointed at a picture of a woman stabbing a man in a bathtub. "It almost looks like a photograph."

Lauren smiled proudly. "It isn't. I painted it. Isn't it nice?"

"It's Charlotte Corday stabbing Marat. She was trying to stop the many executions during the French Revolution," I said.

Kelly rubbed her forehead. "It doesn't need to be in our mural! How will we explain this to the Girl Scout Council? Or the girls who see it?"

I shrugged. "It's an important part of history. And if you think of it, girl empowerment."

The girls were gathered around us, making statements about the quality of the blood spatter.

"And she was executed by guillotine," Lauren said matter-of-factly.

The girls squealed with delight. It made me a little proud to see them cheering on one of my favorite historical characters. The Angel of Assassination, she was called. What Corday had done put in motion the end of The Terror in France.

Kelly stared. "It's not going to be in the mural."

Betty looked up from a guillotine covered in blood that she'd been painting and sighed.

Rex was waiting for me on the couch when I got home. My fiancé patted the seat next to him, so I sat down and leaned my head onto his shoulder.

"Rough meeting?" he asked, putting his arm around me and squeezing.

"Depends on whether you think the French Revolution is an important thing to include in our booth for Thinking Day or not."

It was wonderful leaning against him. It seemed like ages since we'd had a moment alone where we weren't discussing a crime.

Rex's voice was soothing. "If something's up, don't tell me. You and I haven't really had one moment alone that didn't involve work."

He can read minds?

"I know," I said into his chest.

Rex said, "I just realized that today. Between these fires and the missing woman and your stress and sleep disorder, we haven't had any quality time together."

He'd brought up the case, and I was dying to talk to him about it. But he was right. We hadn't had any couple cuddle time in a while.

"How about we just talk about your day?" Rex kissed the top of my head.

My day? I tried to think of something I could discuss besides the Scout meeting, but all I could remember was Riley's weird visit and my trip to the twins' shop to molest a dead cat attached to a robot.

"Just the Scout meeting. We're almost ready for Thinking Day." I told him about Betty's insistence on bloodying up the exhibit.

Rex laughed. "Thank you. I needed a good laugh. You are so lucky to have nothing but this to work on. I envy you."

"Well…" His words grated on me. "It's not like I don't do anything, exactly. And thanks for giving the Fontanas that impression."

He looked surprised. For a moment he didn't respond. "I'm so sorry. I did not mean to imply that you do nothing." Rex pulled me tighter into his embrace. "You mean everything to me, Merry. I can't wait to start our life together."

Now I felt bad for not saying anything about Riley's visit. Or visits. You weren't supposed to keep secrets in a marriage, right? If only they had an etiquette book on that.

"I just want to say how appreciative I am that you're actually staying out of this case." He continued, "Normally you'd be pumping me for intel or begging for clues."

I really felt guilty.

"And now the Feds are getting involved and I…"

With all the fake innocence I could muster, I asked, "The Feds?"

Rex looked tired. Here I was, doing exactly what he was happy about me not doing.

I leaned back. "Sorry. My brain's on autopilot when I hear stuff like that. Forget I said anything."

Rex squeezed me again. "I know it's hard. It's hard for me to not be able to talk to you about my work."

I'd bet it was way harder for me. "Someday we will have to have a real conversation that doesn't include espionage, Girl Scouts, or wedding plans."

"This isn't really your thing. I shouldn't have thrust all the planning on you."

I shook my head. "It's almost done, right? We have the date, the church, the dress. I know we still have to decide where the reception is, but what else is left to do?"

My stomach curdled and my pulse pounded. Oh yeah. I was fine.

I almost forgot! "And, I'm seeing a therapist and participating in a sleep study tonight."

Rex's eyebrows went up. "You're what?"

I nodded. "Kelly lined it up at the hospital. I have to report there at ten in my jammies."

Rex laughed. "I hope you have something other than Dora the Explorer pj's."

Did I? I was enamored with the cartoon—and once had Dora bed sheets as curtains. I always figured Dora was a secret agent and Boots was her handler.

"Come on." He stood and helped me to my feet. "If you're going to do that, we might as well send you with a full stomach. I'm taking you out for pizza."

That was exactly the right thing for him to say. I grabbed my purse, and we walked out the door.

CHAPTER NINTEEN

———

     I sat in my car, wearing my Dora pajamas, staring at the hospital. I've done a lot of strange things in my day, like escaping on a Zamboni in Prague and pretending to be a figure skater from Barbados at the Winter Olympics (needless to say, that didn't go well). But I'd never gone to a hospital and tried to sleep while people stared at me.

     "This has humiliation written all over it," I said to Philby.

     That's right. I brought my cat. It was even harder to relax without her. And if they really wanted to know how I slept, they'd need to see the contortions my body makes as I try to avoid disturbing my obese cat as she lay wherever she wants on the bed. It might be an important key. Besides, if anyone stopped me, I'd say my therapist suggested it. I wasn't entirely sure that would work, but I'd give it a shot.

     Not that it would change anything. Philby wasn't very flexible about our sleeping arrangements.

     Philby jumped up onto the dashboard, and though it was pretty broad, it was like balancing a watermelon on a dowel rod. She fell, rather ungracefully, to the seat and glared at me like it was all my fault.

     In a way, I'm sure it was.

     Scooping up the cat, I exited the car and made my way into the hospital. No one was there this time of night because it was a small town. We didn't have a lot going on. Granted, we did serve all the tiny towns that surrounded us, but this was still a small population.

     I followed the signs that led to the lab.

"Ms. Wrath?" A petite and pretty young woman in a lab coat met me with a smile. "I'm Dr. Tuttle. I'll be helping you through this."

She glanced at my cat and looked like she was about to say something but didn't.

I followed Dr. Tuttle down a dark hallway and into a dimly lit room. A queen-size bed was made up in the middle of the floor, and soft music played. Normally this would've made me relax, but since I was basically a lab rat, I couldn't.

Philby jumped down from my arms and onto the bed. She chose a spot dead center, turned around maybe thirty times, and curled up and closed her eyes.

"Wish I could do that," I mumbled. "I don't suppose you could splice my DNA with cat genes?"

Dr. Tuttle laughed. That made me relax. A little. "Okay, so this is what you designated as your bedtime. Hop into bed and we're off!"

"Shouldn't you hook me up to monitors or something?" I didn't see any wires or electronics.

She shook her head. "That will make it harder for you to fall asleep. For the first time, we try to keep it as natural as possible. We may do that if we need subsequent testing."

I shrugged and pulled back the down comforter. A nightstand stood next to the bed with a bottle of water. That was good. I always slept with water. I wondered how they knew. Maybe I told them. My brain was a little fuzzy.

The fresh flannel sheets were warm and smelled like lavender. This shouldn't be too hard. Right? I slid around the hulking cat in the middle of the bed, fluffed up a pillow, and lay down.

The lights dimmed, but I could still make out a camera on the ceiling directly above me and a two-way mirror across the room. At least I knew who was on the other side of the glass.

My eyes flew open a few minutes—or so I assumed—later. Dr. Tuttle entered the room, closing the door behind her.

"Good morning!"

"Morning?" I blinked as she turned up the lights.

"Yes. You slept a good eight hours without getting up once."

I sat up. Philby was still in her spot from the night before. She refused to wake up when I poked her.

"I can't believe it," I said. "How did that happen?"

Dr. Tuttle smiled. "Sometimes all you need is complete sensory deprivation. Most people charge their phone next to the bed, have animals running around in the night, have cars or trains next to their house. Here, it was dark and silent."

Hmmm…I'd have to change my room to make it dark and soundproof. Would I be able to ban the cats?

"You said you think this is stress-related?" the doctor asked.

"I thought so." I scratched under Philby's chin. The cat came alive. For such a smart, smug animal, she turned into putty if you scratched under her chin.

She continued, "You might have been so tired you just needed a nice, safe place to crash."

"Can I come back tonight?" I asked. Would they let me move in?

"I do want you to come back tonight," Dr. Tuttle said. "We need a second test to make sure the first wasn't a fluke."

I nodded eagerly. Yes! I was going to get two full nights of sleep in a row! I wondered if the doctor would let me high-five her. Deciding against that, I looked meaningfully at Philby. The glare on her face said it all. *Not a chance.*

She hesitated. "One thing…"

Uh-oh. Here it goes. I snore. Or I sleep walk. No wait, she said I never left the bed. What if I gave up classified intel by talking in my sleep? I hadn't worried about that until right then. Was it possible? I braced myself for her response.

"Did you know your cat gets up the minute you fall asleep?"

I shrugged again. "I assume she does. Does it matter?"

The doctor shook her head. "No, it doesn't impact anything. It was just…strange."

Philby was now pretending to be occupied cleaning her paw.

"How so?"

The woman shifted uneasily. "Well, she walked around the room a few times before climbing onto the table next to the two-way mirror. She stared at me for half an hour, tail twitching back and forth. I was sure she could see through the glass. I don't think she even blinked."

Philby continued her charade of suddenly having to clean herself for being very, very dirty.

"You're joking."

"Then she tapped on the window, meowed at me, and went back to the bed. Just before curling up and closing her eyes, she looked directly at the camera overhead and meowed very loudly."

My cat was so weird. And awesome!

"That *is* bizarre." I nodded, wondering what to do with this information. "I don't have to bring her back tonight," I said.

Dr. Tuttle's eyebrows went up. "Please bring her back. She makes the time pass much more quickly."

I walked out of the hospital into daylight, still wearing my pajamas, still carrying an obese cat.

"Good girl," I whispered. She had my back. Who needs a dog?

Philby ignored me.

Back at home, Martini charged us like a bull. She ran circles around both her mother and me before sitting in front of us, meowing loudly for five minutes. Since she looks like Elvis, it was a little strange to be chewed out by the fur ball. When she was done, she turned tail and headed back down the hallway to the bedroom.

After a quick shower and some breakfast, I dialed the number I'd found in the vacuum cleaner. No one answered, and there was a recording that said the owner hadn't set up a voicemail account yet. I ran a search of the number online but came up empty. I'd just have to keep trying.

I still had another avenue of investigation and sat down with Kate's laptop to try again. Maybe with a clear head and a full night's sleep, I could make sense of all those cat pictures.

Who takes only cat pictures? I don't even have one on my cell phone. Wait...did that make me a bad cat mom?

The pictures of the dead cat, featuring him very much alive, filled the screen. One by one, I went over them again, looking for clues in the background...a notepad with writing, a calendar...anything.

Did this make me seem crazy? Studying photos I'd already examined. Was this part of my madness? A seed of doubt crept into my mind. Maybe there wasn't anything going on. Maybe Kate was just a weirdo with a safe room and a cat fetish. Maybe the Fontanas weren't spies—just socially awkward.

Like a house of cards that falls after one mistake, my whole theory crashed to the floor. The eight hours of sleep must've allowed me to regain control of my brain, using real reasoning. It was possible I'd been a paranoid nutcase. The insomnia had made me crazy. I really should make another appointment with Susan before I started killing my cats and having them stuffed and attached to appliances.

I thought about what Susan had said. *Sometimes things look one way, but underneath is something very different. While this might not be the main reason for your insomnia, it might be one piece of the puzzle.*

She was so smart. The only thing that bothered me was how she found out about Rex. I could be making too much out of it. Or things had layers, which she'd said. She...

But underneath is something very different...

I pulled the laptop closer and opened one of the cat pictures. What was I saying? They're all cat pictures. In this particular photo, an angry Mr. Pickles was sitting in an Easter basket wearing giant bunny ears. That would do.

Next, I searched the programs installed in the software. How did I not see this before? I was an idiot! Okay, maybe not an idiot, but rusty. This was steganography. A method of hiding information underneath layers of color in a picture. And there it was—a special program used to layer photographs. I'd seen this before. These programs were unique, usually coded by the user. But they all ran on the same principle of a complicated photoshopping program.

I began to strip away colors embedded in the cat photo. It took a long time. You had to know which components of which colors to remove. Whoever Kate Becks was messaging knew which layers to strip. Kate knew it. I did not.

The work was painfully slow, and I'd be lying if I said I didn't curse once or thirty-five times. Minutes turned into hours. I took a break for lunch to clear my head, hoping for some inspiration from the Pizza Rolls and ranch dressing. No such luck.

As I worked through the afternoon, I started figuring it out. The curves and angles of letters began to appear. At least it was English. I could speak Russian and Spanish, but it would be easier not to have to translate.

If only Riley was here. He was great at cryptography and a master of this particular brand of steganography. Then again, I was still mad at him. Besides, figuring this out on my own would be good for me.

By dinnertime, I'd gotten it down to where I could at least read through the last layer.

I'm being followed. They know.

I leaned back in my chair, exhausted. This was only one message out of dozens. And while it got easier as I went along, did I really want to spend the next week decoding each and every photo?

At least I had some wine in the house. I poured a glass of red and stared at the message. It proved, to me at least, that Kate was a spy. She was talking about being made and someone following her. She must have been collecting information for someone…but what? For whom?

I leaned back in my chair, suddenly weary as I looked at the other dozens of photos. And while it got easier as I went along, did I really want to spend the next week decoding each and every photo? Did I want to stare at Mr. Pickles' sour face over and over?

I should give the laptop to Rex. They had a whole computer forensics team in Des Moines who could uncover all these messages in no time.

It would prove to my fiancé that I was capable of making the right decisions. That I understood the importance of his job. That I was putting my past behind me.

Pulling my cell out of my pocket, I called across the street.

There was no answer. Huh. It was almost eight o'clock. What was he up to? I tried again, every twenty minutes, until I had to get ready to go back to the sleep study. Rex texted back, asking me to quit calling and saying all was well, that he was just at work. Feeling better, I changed into my pj's, grabbed my rotund cat, and headed out.

Dr. Tuttle greeted me again, and I was shown to the same bed. Philby curled up in the middle of it and zonked out. As I drifted off, I tried to remember what else Susan had said. She'd made it sound like I needed to find myself. Kind of. I guess. With my last conscious thought, I decided she was right.

Something was wrong, my brain told me. Opening my eyes, I saw it was completely dark. Philby wasn't on the bed. This could've been a dream.

Bang!

Something slammed against the two-way mirror, and I sprang out of bed. Philby! As I waited for my eyes to adjust to the gloom, I carefully worked my way over in the direction of the sound.

Something furry rubbed up against my legs, and I sighed with relief. Philby was okay. Picking up the cat, I deposited her onto the bed and climbed back in. I was so drowsy. That was good because I wanted to sleep. If I did it right, they wouldn't need me to come back. I'd just keep seeing my therapist, and eventually I could end that too.

My eyes closed, and I had the sensation of floating into the darkness. It was nice.

Thump.

My eyes flew open. For a soundproof environment, this place was failing. Perhaps this was part of the test—to see how I'd do with distractions? That made sense, and I closed my eyes again.

Philby shifted on the bed, and I heard her jump down to the floor. She was investigating. That would give Dr. Tuttle another great story.

Scrape...

That sounded like a shoe. Someone was in here with me. That seemed unprofessional. I opened my eyes. The sound of metal on leather sent my heart pounding. I knew that sound. It was the sound of a knife being taken from a leather sheaf. It was on my right.

I rolled over to the left just as something made contact with the pillow next to me. I landed on my feet and waited to hear footfalls, or someone bumping into the bed.

It was completely silent. I ran my hands over the sheets and came away with a handful of feathers. Someone had stabbed my pillow. And they'd thought they'd connect with my head.

Why stab someone in the head? It's not like it was easy. The skull made it harder. There were lots of squishier places where you could do a lot more damage quickly. As these thoughts rambled around my head, I continued to listen for any sound at all. Nothing.

My eyes adjusted a little, and I could make out the dark shape of a person still standing on the other side of the bed. Whoever it was, my attacker hadn't moved. Thoughts would be racing through his mind. Had he missed by inches? Had I shifted in the bed and he just had to find me? If I were him, I'd realize I only had one more shot at this.

Someone had tried to kill me.

Where was Philby? If I had to guess, I'd say she wasn't in immediate danger. Cats knew their way around in the dark. I'd like to think she'd lay low, realizing what kind of situation this was.

"Ms. Wrath?" A vaguely familiar female voice—with an outrageous Southern accent added in an attempt to disguise it—came from the other side of the bed. "You can get up now. We're having some trouble with the lights. Tell me where you are."

I said nothing. The shoe scraped against the floor again. My assailant was walking around the head of the bed. Fortunately, I was barefoot and able to move silently. As I made my way slowly around the foot of the bed, the two of us changed sides.

Crouching low on the floor so she wouldn't see me but I could see her feet, I held my breath.

"I know you're here," the woman said. "You couldn't have gone out. Not without me noticing. Please let me know you're all right."

So you can stab me? No way.

I needed a plan. The attacker would run out of patience and probably find the light switch. I needed a weapon. But unless I was going to garrote her with my Dora the Explorer pajamas, I was out of ideas.

The theory was, rush a gun, run from a knife. A gun makes noise, and if it does shoot you, others will come to see what happened—which was great news since I was already in a hospital.

But a knife… A knife could do irreparable damage. And silently.

I did a mental assessment of the room, but there wasn't anything in it I could use. Not that I could see, anyway.

"Ms. Wrath!" the voice snapped. "You are wasting our time! I know you're not in this bed. Speak up so we can take the next step!"

Oh sure, considering the next step was her knife going into my soft body, I decided to keep quiet. She was still standing on the other side of the bed. An idea popped into my head.

With all my might, I shoved the bed as hard as I could and just kept pushing. A grunt came from the other side, but I didn't stop. With luck, I could smash her between the bed and wall, which would give me enough time to hit the lights, grab Philby, and get out of there.

The bed groaned as I pushed it across the tile floor. It was still heavy, so I knew she was still there. I couldn't stop and give her time to get around the bed because now Knifey McKnife Face knew exactly where I was.

I heard a loud yowl, followed by a hiss, and it stopped me in my tracks. My assailant was running toward the door. It opened, and all I could see was the backlit shadow of the woman as she closed the door and ran down the hallway.

It took me a moment to reach the light switch. Blinded for a moment, I blinked to see Philby nursing her front right paw. The woman had stepped on her. I found my phone on the dresser and was about to dial 9-1-1, when a thought occurred to me. I hit the number I'd dialed from the slip of paper. In the distance, a phone went off. My attacker had that number—the number Kate had hidden in the Roomba.

"Dr. Tuttle?" I shouted. No answer.

Philby was hot on my heels as I flung open the door and ran to the observation area. The door was open, and I saw Dr. Tuttle slumped over a table in front of the two-way mirror. On the wall was a button—a panic button for the security team. I hit it and turned my attention to the fallen woman.

The doctor was breathing and still had a pulse. I waited with her until help arrived in the form of the hospital's security team and a couple of nurses.

"How does this keep happening?" Rex said from behind me. Wow. He got there fast.

I turned and fell into his arms, remaining there until my heartbeat slowed to normal.

"You were just in a sleep study, right?" Rex's voice rumbled through his chest.

I pulled back and looked at him. "I had nothing to do with this."

I explained the whole scenario—how I'd been attacked, how the attacker got away (leaving out the part about the phone number). He listened carefully and took notes.

Hey! I was an *actual* victim! This was what it was like to be legitimately interviewed by the police! It was kind of nice, actually. Usually I'm apologizing for getting involved in something or lying about getting involved in something.

But I hadn't done anything wrong.

Awesome!

Dr. Tuttle came to, unable to describe who smashed her forehead into the two-way glass. She was far more concerned with me than herself. Which was nice. The forensics team came in and started working on both rooms.

Rex pulled me aside. "You're not quite out of the woods, you know."

"What do you mean?"

"No one randomly attacks a sleep study patient. You've been digging into all of this. Haven't you?" His eyebrows went up.

Busted.

"Yeah." I slumped. "You're right. Can you stop by my house when you're done here? I'll explain." I was tired of all of this. Philby gave me a look that said she agreed.

Rex shook his head. "No. You are staying right here until I'm done. Then, I'm driving you home and you can explain."

I looked through the mirror at the bed on the other side. I kind of wanted to go back to it until Rex was ready to leave. But since I'd used that bed as a weapon, they were likely checking it for evidence.

Philby and I sat off to the side while the police swarmed the rooms. I examined the cat. Her paw was sore but not broken. I'd have to keep my eye on that. I could take her to see Dr. Alvarez.

With Philby's injury, the last thing I wanted to do was continue investigating. A weariness draped over me like a lead cape. This mystery was wearing me out. With the wedding, my troop, my mother's visit, and meeting Rex's sisters, I no longer cared about the stupid spies who really might not be spies next door.

Once Rex sat down with me, I'd tell him everything and turn over the laptop. From this moment on, I was through with being an amateur detective. I was done with therapists and sleep studies. From here on out I was just going to focus on my girls, my cats, and the wedding.

Philby purred from my lap. It was so soothing. I leaned my head back against the wall and closed my eyes.

"Merry?" Rex was standing over me, gently shaking my shoulders.

I blinked. I was still in the hospital. Philby was still on my lap. What time was it? How long had I been out?

Rex helped me to my feet, taking Philby and tucking her under his arm. "I'd better get you home."

"No," I said groggily. "We need to talk. I need to tell you stuff."

"That can wait a couple of hours. I've got to get back and wrap things up here. I'm swamped."

He guided me to his car and put my cat and me inside.

"Okay. But come over as soon as that's over and I can fill you in on things." I yawned.

"You got it."

Rex left as soon as he'd tucked me into my bed. To my surprise, I passed out instantly.

A noise woke me up. How much time had gone by? I checked my cell. I'd been out for five hours.

In the distance, a door closed. It sounded like the front door. I got out of bed and stumbled toward the hallway. Rex must be back. He'd let himself in and was letting me get a few zzz's.

The sound of kitchen drawers being opened and shut made me pause just shy of my bedroom door. What if it wasn't Rex? What if it was the woman who'd attacked me and she was here to finish the job? She was certainly in the right room, considering her interest in knives.

Very carefully, I reached over to the closet door and pulled out a shotgun. I didn't keep it loaded. If my troop found it, there'd be all kinds of holes in this house. The safe in the back of the closet was set for my biometrics. I pressed all five fingers down, and seconds later, the door opened.

It is not easy to load a shotgun quietly. Oh sure, why not use a handgun, you say? Pshaw. Don't get me wrong—I'm a crack shot with a pistol. But only when I'm wide awake. A shotgun is much better for hitting your target when you aren't fully in the moment.

Sliding the last cartridge into the gun, I leaned against the doorway and glanced out. The sound of cupboard doors opening and closing told me that unless Rex was cooking something that used every implement in my kitchen, I was dealing with an intruder.

The laptop!

My mind raced to remember what I'd done with it. Obviously it wasn't sitting in plain sight, or the intruder wouldn't be searching the kitchen. So where did I put it?

Philby trotted up the hallway toward me. She didn't seem alarmed. Which meant it was someone she knew. I relaxed and slumped against the door. It had to be Rex. And he must be making breakfast.

I snapped the safety on and shouldered my weapon. It didn't hurt to take it with me…just in case.

As I turned into the kitchen, I froze.

"Riley! What are you doing here?"

My former partner froze. He was surrounded by every pot, pan, and dish in my house. The cupboards and drawers were all open. I lifted my shotgun and aimed at his heart. I wasn't going to kill him, but scaring him was a definite option.

Riley's casual smile wavered a fraction when he saw the shotgun but went back to his usual, annoying expression.

"I was going to make breakfast."

I was fully awake now. "Oh yeah? Where's the food?"

"I hadn't gotten it out yet. I wanted to make sure you had everything I needed. And seriously, Wrath, your organization is a mess."

Out of the corner of my eye, I spotted the laptop on the fridge. He hadn't noticed it yet.

"Sit." I waved the shotgun at the chairs at the breakfast bar.

We exchanged places so that he sat and I stood in the kitchen. I lowered the shotgun and took the laptop down from the fridge. Riley's eyes widened a fraction of a millimeter. So that *was* what he was after.

"You *are* investigating something here, you liar."

Riley didn't take his eyes off the laptop. "May I see that?"

"No." I shook my head. "You lied to me."

"Look…" He ran his fingers through his wavy blond hair. "I'm just doing my job. You're not in the CIA anymore, and you've never been a Fed, so this isn't something you need to know. Hand me the laptop."

I was saving the laptop for Rex. But to be honest, Rex would just have to hand it over to the FBI if espionage was involved. Still, I should be more loyal to my fiancé.

I held the laptop against my chest. "Tell me what you think you're going to find on it."

"Tell me what you found on it." Riley's face was completely blank.

We were at an impasse. I hated impasses. They always ended with a shootout. Always.

I took one step closer to the breakfast bar to give him a bit of hope. "You tell me whose laptop you think this is, and I'll consider it."

Riley sighed. Behind his calm demeanor, I knew he was wrestling with what to do here.

"I won't jeopardize your job," I said. "I just want to know if I'm right."

He seemed conflicted. "I can't tell you."

I backed up toward the fridge. "Alright. I'll send it to the newspaper with everything I know."

Riley paled. "The *Des Moines Register*?"

He had reason to worry. Most people not from Iowa didn't know that the *Register* was a hard-hitting, Pulitzer Prize winning paper. They'd get to the bottom of it in no time, and the FBI would have a public relations nightmare on their hands.

Riley didn't need to know that I was actually thinking of the local paper. I saw the arguments at war in his head. He might think he had one over on me, but he most likely had his doubts. I was becoming more unpredictable to him.

"Okay," he said finally. "We think Kate Becks was a double agent. She worked with us, but the Russians thought she was with them. Her disappearance has us all a bit nervous."

It wasn't easy to keep the snark out of my voice. "Because maybe she was a double for their side, not ours?"

Riley nodded. "She dropped off the radar a few days ago. We searched her place, but…"

I finished his sentence for him. "The local police arrived and scared you off."

Wow. I'd investigated after the FBI and the police. They hadn't found the secret room. I kind of wanted to brag about that a little.

"How did you know about the laptop? How did you know I had it?"

Riley grinned. "Because I know you. I knew you thought your neighbors were illegals. I followed you to see you go to

Kate Becks' place of employment and where she was getting therapy. You'd put two and two together. I figured if there was any intel—you'd find it."

"I'm not sure how to take that." Was he complimenting me or insulting me? "Wait! You tricked me into working for the FBI!"

Riley stood and walked around the breakfast bar. I thought about shooting him but decided instead to set the gun down.

"You're not FBI," he said as he stood unnervingly close to me. "But investigating and espionage are in your blood. You're just like me." Riley reached up and tucked a stray curl behind my ear. "We make a good team."

Steeling myself, I pushed him away. "If we make such a good team, why didn't you share intel with me?"

To be honest, his nearness had a small effect on me. Riley was one of those men who could charm the panties off even the coldest ice queen. I'd be lying if parts of me (which shall remain nameless) didn't react to his touch.

He stepped back, and the spell was broken. "Because this isn't your case. It's ours."

"And the local police, who've been investigating her disappearance? Don't you have to wait to see what they are willing to share?"

Riley grimaced. "We were going to tell them, once we had the laptop."

"Sit…" I pointed back to the barstool. "And let me think about this."

Riley went back to his chair and waited.

On the one hand, I should hand this over to Rex. If I didn't, he'd question my loyalty. In the back of my mind, I've always suspected that Rex was concerned about Riley's presence in my life. He knew about our past relationship, professional and otherwise.

On the other hand, technically, this was a case for the FBI. They investigated spies. They had every right to this information. And lastly—I really, really wanted to know what was going on.

I opted for Team Rex and called to invite him over. Riley frowned, but I figured this was fair. Both agencies would get the intelligence together. I was off the hook. Kind of. I was pretty sure both men wouldn't like this idea.

Rex walked in the door minutes later. His eyebrows went up when he saw Riley, but he said nothing.

"This is Kate Becks' laptop." I opened it up and turned it on. "Since both of you are investigating this case, I figured both of you should have my information at the same time."

Rex and Riley said nothing. Yep. They were mad.

"Riley's with the FBI and investigating Kate because she was a double agent for them."

Riley narrowed his eyes at me but continued his silence.

I pointed at my fiancé. "Rex is investigating the disappearance of a local woman, and I suspect the fires are part of this."

I pulled up the screen with the message and turned it toward them.

"It's steganography," I said.

Riley's eyes grew wide. Rex looked at me curiously, so I explained.

"There are a ton of cat pictures on this. It took me all day to uncover one message. But you—" I pointed at Riley "— should be able to decode the rest fairly quickly."

Riley stood and scooped up the laptop. "Thank you for your assistance. The FBI appreciates it."

I shook my head. "Nope. You're going to do it here, where Rex and I can see it."

"I can't do that. This whole thing is classified. And you're both civilians," he complained. "No offense."

Rex finally spoke up. "I need to see proof that this is a case for the Feds. I can't turn it over to you until I know for sure." He turned to me. "Where did you get this?"

I had no choice but to tell them both how I broke into the house, found the secret room, and took the computer. Rex listened without questions, but the vein in his forehead told me we'd be discussing this later.

"How did you get in there?" Riley asked. He sounded annoyed. "We left when we saw the police coming."

I shrugged. "You left the front door open. I didn't see you either. You must have been in another room or the garage when I was inside. Does it matter?"

From the wounded look on his face, I was guessing it did. His pride was injured because he'd missed my arrival on the scene. Oh for crying out loud! Men are so ridiculous!

Riley looked from Rex to me. With a sigh he sat back down, opened the laptop, and went to work. I started putting things back in the cupboards. While I knew Riley would be able to decipher the pictures faster than I had, it would still take a while.

Rex sat at the breakfast bar and watched. His silence was unnerving. I wanted to ask about the investigation at the hospital, but I knew he wouldn't say anything in front of Riley. Plus, I didn't want Riley to know about the attack during the sleep study.

These two men were so different, and yet the same. I knew them both intimately. And that was the problem. And furthermore, Rex wanted to marry me. Riley did not. But he was definitely interested in rekindling our romance.

That's where the comparisons ended. Riley was spontaneous and reckless and often lied to me, where Rex was mature, trusting, and safe. At one time, my life fit with Riley's. Being a spy, you rarely go by the book...whatever book that might be.

Now, however, I was more like Rex. Okay, not maturity-wise. But I liked living in my small hometown. I loved my Girl Scout troop and my sometimes-boring life that was sandwiched between dead bodies every now and then.

Rex had been the right choice, and I truly loved him. That didn't mean I still didn't feel all squirmy over Riley whenever he burst into my life. I tried to picture a life with him, but all I came up with was total chaos.

With this realization, I relaxed. My fears about the wedding faded. I knew what I was doing. And I was doing the right thing. I wanted to marry Rex.

The kitchen had been put back together, and Riley was halfway through the pictures. Because silence makes me a bit edgy, I thought of a question I could ask Rex.

"Do you think Kate vanished of her own accord, or is she dead?"

Riley looked up. "If she is alive, I need to find her. But I'm starting to think she's dead."

Rex shook his head. "She's not dead until we find a body."

I pressed on. "In your years of experience, what do you think?"

My fiancé scowled. "My experience tells me that she's alive until proven dead."

I threw my hands up into the air. "What do you need for proof?"

"A body," Rex said again.

"Riley"—I turned to the other man—"how are the Fontanas involved? Are they illegals?"

My former handler studied my fiancé. "I can't say."

There was some sort of male posturing going on here. Like two roosters with puffed-out chests, each trying to take over the henhouse. And that henhouse was me. What did that make Philby, I wondered?

"I think she was spying on the Fontanas," I said at last. "They found out and killed her."

Rex rubbed his eyes. "Merry, I can't work off speculation like that. I need evidence."

"I gave you evidence the other night, when I called you to say I'd seen Mark and Pam with a body," I snapped.

Riley suppressed a grin, but I knew it was there.

"How do the fires link with this?" I asked.

Rex sighed. "We haven't really found any links. All of the arson cases look like they were the work of teenagers with cigarettes. The fire at Kate Becks' house was started with accelerant."

"Teenagers with cigarettes? Are you joking?"

"No. We've found a lighter and cigarettes at each scene. At one of the locations we found a six-pack of cheap beer."

"That doesn't make sense," I mused. "I mean, I can see it happening once with a bunch of kids, but twice?"

"There is another option," Rex reasoned. "That the fires were all set to make it look like the later fire at the Becks house was just another case of arson."

"That sounds more like it," I agreed. "This wouldn't be the first time a criminal committed several crimes to cover one."

Rex nodded.

I turned to the ex-CIA former boyfriend. "But Riley, you still haven't answered my question about the Fontanas."

"I'm busy," he said without looking up from the computer.

"Okay, how about this? Why would there be so many spies in Who's There, Iowa?"

"That's where your case falls apart, Merry," Rex said. "It doesn't make any sense. There isn't anything I can think of that would attract spies, unless it was in Des Moines. And if that was true, why didn't the spies settle there? It's easier to blend into the woodwork in a big city…"

"…but they'd stand out in a small town," I finished.

"I don't think the Fontanas are guilty of anything but living next door to you," Rex said.

"I've got something," Riley announced.

Instead of taking this argument to the next level, we crowded around the screen. We scanned through dozens of messages, all very short. The gist? Kate was convinced that she was being followed. She thought she was in jeopardy. That would explain why she fled.

"Were these messages meant for you?" I asked Riley.

"If so," he answered, "we didn't see them."

"So, it's possible she could've doubled but on the side of the Fontanas. These messages were for them." I pointed to a batch of cat pictures. "What about those?"

Riley waved at the screen. "They're just pictures of her cat. No steganography there."

That made sense, I supposed. My screen saver is an extreme close-up of Philby, staring into the lens on my laptop.

"Let's imagine she's working with the Russians." I waved off Riley when he looked about to protest. "Just spitballing. Could the Fontanas be her contacts?"

Rex said, "Then why kill her?"

"Maybe she was going to start batting for the other side," I suggested. What was with all the baseball metaphors? I didn't watch baseball.

"Or"—Riley rubbed his chin—"the Fontanas are exactly who they say they are and she's referring to the FBI closing in. She probably realized we'd be onto her sooner or later."

"And yet, you missed it," I said smugly.

Riley ignored me. "We aren't investigating your neighbors."

I leaned against the bar. That took the wind out of my sails. Maybe I was just being paranoid. Maybe I was hallucinating. It's been a weird week. Anything was possible. I needed to make another appointment with Susan.

I thought about the phone number I'd gotten at Ferguson Taxidermy. If I handed it over, Riley would know I was attacked, and I didn't want that kind of attention from him. He needed to work with Rex from here on out and leave me alone. I opted to say nothing. After all, I couldn't find out who it belonged to, so they wouldn't be able to either.

"Alright," I said, "if the FBI is following her and she felt threatened, where would she go?"

No one spoke. It looked like I was the one who knew this woman best. She wouldn't go back to her job. They'd go there first. She couldn't go to her house, because it was burned to the ground. Where do you hide in a town like this?

Riley got up and closed the laptop. "Satisfied? I need to talk to my team."

Rex nodded and also stood. "I'd better get back to work."

Oh good. That would postpone the argument I was sure we were going to have.

As I watched them go, even though they were handling everything now, I couldn't help but wonder about the missing woman. Unlike Rex, I wouldn't rule out that she was dead. That was still on the table. And if she was dead, where was her body? And if she was alive, where was she?

CHAPTER TWENTY

Two days passed with no contact from Riley and very little from Rex. That was fine with me. I was no longer on the case.

Thinking Day had arrived. As Kelly and I stood near our tables on France, the girls—looking adorable in their berets, pink shirts, black pants, and ballet flats—were setting up the craft area.

They really were cute. Betty had arrived wearing a shirt that said *Freedom for the Basque People*. I thought that was fine because she was right. Kelly made her switch. Betty responded by drawing a mustache over her lip.

"Where'd she get a Sharpie?" I asked as I tried scrubbing it off.

Kelly searched the girl and found the contraband marker in her back pocket.

"This isn't coming off," I said. "She'll just have to wear a mustache."

"Theeez eez moi being zee auzenteec," the girl said in a mangled French accent.

I turned around and realized that all the other girls now had permanent mustaches.

"Zeees eeez zee zoleedarity." Lauren nodded gravely.

Fortunately this time, the facial hair was made with a Bic.

"Let their parents deal with this," I said to Kelly, who looked like she was going to explode.

"But they don't look so cute anymore," my best friend lamented.

"Drop the accents, girls," I said. "People need to understand you."

The girls agreed. They kind of looked grateful.

"Doors are opening in five minutes," a Council member onstage warned. "You've all done a terrific job, ladies!" She spotted Betty with her mustache, and her mouth dropped open.

"Remember…" Kelly gathered the girls around her. "We are here to inform and teach these girls about France. Got it?"

The girls nodded and took up positions. The Kaitlyns would be handing out éclairs and sparkling apple cider to mimic French champagne. The Hannahs were in charge of helping the girls make little flags for the SWAPS. Emily, Caterina, Inez, and Ava were going to teach a little folk dance I suspected they'd made up.

"Hey," I asked Kelly, "where's Betty?"

We found her at the table for Spain, handing out flyers in support of the Catalans and Basque people.

"We need to end the oppression by the Spanish and French overlords!" Betty wailed.

Most of the girls stared at her with mouths open. One little girl nodded in agreement. The leaders looked confused.

"Catalans?" one of the women asked.

After apologizing, I led Betty back to the girls and installed her with the Hannahs.

"Oh no!" Kelly shrieked. "I left the safety pins for the SWAPS in the car!"

I calmed her down. "I'll get them." I took her keys and set out.

It would be wrong not to inspect the other tables as I walked by. It's always good to know your enemy…I mean…competition. To my delight, not one other table looked like ours—probably because we took up a whole corner with five tables.

What the…? I stopped dead in my tracks. A group of Brownies were huddled around a table that had a huge sign that said *Hamas*! Were terrorists recruiting Girl Scouts? Diabolical! The girls were holding plastic bags that said *Army of One*. What was happening?

I wove my way through the crowd to get closer. Who approved a table for a militant terrorist group? It had to be Juliette Dowd. She probably put a hit on my table. Unbelievable! I should…

Wait…

An adult near the display moved, and I saw that it was really *Bahamas*. That was a relief. I really was tired. Did I really think the Girl Scout Council would approve a table for a terrorist organization?

Focus, Merry! Kelly needs those pins. As I walked out the door, swimming against the wave of little girls and their leaders, I realized I should've taken a picture when it said *HAMAS*. That would've made a great Christmas card.

Kelly's car was parked next to mine—at the back of the lot. A sea of minivans made it a bit harder to remember exactly where I'd parked. When we'd arrived, there was no one else here. Now it was kind of like the Mall of America on Black Friday.

When I'd narrowed it down to about thirty silver minivans, I hit the trunk release on Kelly's keys. One trunk flipped open. Awesome. What an amazing invention. If only I'd had that technology back in Cairo, when I had to find my camel out of three dozen.

I spotted the large gallon baggies filled with pins and bent over to grab them, when someone came up behind me and shoved a washcloth in my mouth. Chloroform! I'd know it anywhere. I struggled to fight as the world slowly spun into black. My last thought was how was Kelly going to get the pins?

CHAPTER TWENTY-ONE

———

There was a slapping sound. It seemed to come from a mile away. My eyes felt like they'd been glued shut, and when I tried to move it felt like I was swimming in water.

I wasn't. I'd have known if I was wet. Gradually sensation crept back into my sore limbs. There was some vague pain in my wrists and ankles. The weight of my body told me I was tied to a chair.

I forced my eyes open. They wanted to stay shut. They might as well have been, because I still couldn't see. I was blind! Wait…nope. It was just a blindfold. Bound and blindfolded. Was I gagged too?

It's kind of a misconception—being gagged. If you're a spy and you've been kidnapped, it's rare to be forced into silence. Bad guys kidnapped you because they wanted information from you. They *wanted* you to talk.

Licking my lips, I realized there was no such restraint. My mouth was uncovered. Yup. Someone wanted me to answer some questions.

Good luck with that I thought, as I strained to listen. I wasn't saying a word voluntarily. It wasn't totally quiet. Someone had a radio on in the distance. It sounded like that weird music they used to play in elevators. Easy listening with no annoying lyrics, which was still annoying. I thought I could hear strains from "The Girl From Ipanema," but I might have been imagining it.

Someone was walking toward me. From the slap of rubber on cement and the heavy footfall, I figured it was a man. The sound stopped right in front of me. I figured whoever it was, was only a foot or so away.

He was breathing quickly. Like he was nervous. Well, he should be. This bastard took me away from my troop on Thinking Day! Didn't he know how much work had gone into that?

I tested my restraints. Rope. And rough rope at that. That sucked. Coarse fibers tore into my skin as I tensed and relaxed my arms. Why couldn't it have been zip ties? Or handcuffs? I could get free of those. Inch-thick rope, however, would be difficult.

And why wasn't he saying anything? That wasn't a good sign. He was probably going to smack me around first to loosen my tongue. I could handle that. What I didn't like, was knives. I really didn't like the idea of being tortured with knives.

My captor turned and walked away. His footsteps echoed on the floor for a long time. When they stopped, I heard whispering. Someone else was here. I strained to listen, but all I heard was mumbling.

This had to be related to the mysterious disappearance of Kate Becks. It had to be. Why take me otherwise? Of course, it could be someone from my past career. But there were so many enemies there, it would be hard to find out who.

No, I was basically undercover here in Iowa. Only the CIA knew I was here.

The whispering continued, but the noise was too soft. I dropped forward, slouching as if I'd passed out. Would they buy it?

By the way, I wouldn't recommend doing that. My body weight strained my arms as they held me to the chair. If it worked, however, I could at least get a clue as to who my captors were. They'd better hurry up, though. My arms and wrists couldn't take much more.

My efforts were rewarded as I heard two sets of footsteps heading my way. I couldn't tell if the other set belonged to a man or woman. But it really didn't matter at this point.

"What happened?" A woman whose voice and bad accent I remembered from that stabby night at the sleep study spoke. She was trying to disguise it so I had no idea who she really was.

"Maybe I gave her too much chloroform?" the man asked in a fake English accent, also attempting to disguise his voice.

Neither of them was very good at it because I knew these weren't their natural voices. Still, it was enough to throw me off. And that was all they needed to do.

"How much did you use?" the woman asked.

"I followed the instructions on the package."

It took everything I had not to laugh.

The woman shrieked, "You must've used too much. How long do you think she'll be out?"

"I don't know. I've never chloroformed anyone before. You know that," the man grumbled.

So this was a couple who worked together regularly. It didn't sound like my neighbors, but I couldn't rule it out.

"How do we wake her up?" she asked.

"Let's check the package. It might say how long she'll be out."

The two walked away. They had a package with instructions? How silly. My troop would be better spies than these idiots.

From a distance the conversation continued.

"We could throw water on her to bring her around. Or," the man said, "I've got the stun gun in the trunk of the car."

I sat up. "I can hear you," I shouted. I could handle torture, but it was too cold in the building to be doused with water, and I wasn't terribly fond of stun guns.

"Ms. Wrath…" The woman's voice gained confidence as she came closer. "Your timing is perfect."

"Yours isn't." My voice sounded like gravel. "I've got somewhere I'm supposed to be right now."

"If you answer the questions," she said, "we might let you go back there."

"Somehow I doubt that," I snapped.

"You're probably right," the woman sneered. "It's far more likely you'll end up in a dumpster somewhere when we're done here."

"Well," I said through gritted teeth, "let's get this over with, then."

A fist connected with my jawbone, and my head flew backward.

"Hey!" I wanted to massage my throbbing jaw but couldn't. "I didn't say I wouldn't cooperate!"

That was going to leave a mark.

The fist struck me in the cheek this time, sending waves of pain through my head.

"Stop that!" I said.

A hand slapped me hard. This was getting ridiculous.

I flexed my jaw. "What's the point of torturing me before you ask your questions?"

The man laughed. "You watch too much TV. Spies aren't predictable."

Spies. They get dumber every day.

"Civilians," the woman said, "they get dumber every day."

That's what *they* thought. Still, telling them that wouldn't help me right now. It was better for them to think they were superior. For the moment, they didn't need to know that I wasn't predictable either.

"Okay," I said slowly, "what is it you want to know?"

"Where's the laptop?" the man shouted.

Ah. Definitely part of this case. Here was the dilemma. Did I tell them I gave it to the authorities or not? If I tell them I don't have it, they could let me go, thinking I'm just some rube. On the other hand, they could kill me and drop my body in a dumpster. I was pretty good at reading people, but these two hadn't given me enough to work with yet.

I went with rube.

"If I tell you, will you let me go? I couldn't even get into it. The password was protected," I whined, hoping I sounded helpless.

The fist connected once again with my jaw in an uppercut that made my teeth hurt.

"Stop doing that!" the woman hissed. "How's she going to answer if you break her jaw?"

The man mumbled something unintelligible but desisted.

"Tell us where it is, and we will let you go," the woman purred.

She was lying. The minute I coughed up the location of the laptop, I was a dead woman. Ironic, right? So many people had died around me that I guess it was just a matter of time.

I didn't answer. My mind was working through my options as quickly as it could.

"I really will let you go," the woman said sweetly. "I'd hate for your sweet, adorable kitty to starve to death because you never came home."

She knew about my cats. It *had* to be Mark and Pam Fontana. Then again, these two could just be following me. That's how they knew I was in a sleep study. I took Philby, so they knew I had a cat.

A cat… A *cat*!

"Okay, okay! I'll tell you!" I lied. "Please don't kill me!"

As a stalling technique, I resorted to sobbing. Loudly.

"I just want to go home!" I cried. "Please don't hurt me or my cat."

"You mean cats, don't you?" the man corrected.

Gotcha.

I was very good at crying at will. My graduating class at the Farm voted me "Best Crier." My tears leaked out from under my blindfold, and I took big gulps of air so I'd look like I was hyperventilating.

"Calm down," the woman I now knew was Pam said. "Look what you've done!" she shrieked at her partner.

"What I've done? How did I do this?" Mark argued. "You're the one who had to bring up death and dumpsters and threatening her cats." He muttered under his breath, "Stupid cats. I hate cats."

"*You take that back!*" Pam Fontana screamed.

"*No!*" Mark returned the scream. "You like cats more than you like me!"

Ping! An alarm went off in my brain as it all came together. It all made sense now. The missing woman, the dead cat on a vacuum cleaner, the laptop filled with cat pictures. My neighbors.

I needed to get them to untie me. I needed a distraction.

With a final, loud wail, I flung the chair sideways until it and I landed on the floor. I froze, feigning unconsciousness for the second time. Something wet and warm trickled down the side of my face. Awesome! I'd managed to injure myself. That was just what I needed!

"You killed her!" Pam was so distracted, she didn't even try to disguise her voice.

"I didn't kill her!" Mark dropped the strange voice too.

"Yes you did! It's because you hate cats!" Pam shrieked.

I just lay there in a small puddle of blood, listening.

"I think she's breathing." Mark felt close.

He must've been kneeling. I felt his hands working on the ropes around my wrists and ankles. I remained very still. Even when he lifted me off the floor and carried me to something soft, like a sofa or a bed.

I remained totally limp. My timing had to be perfect. I was still blindfolded, and I needed to be able to see.

"She's bleeding from the head," Pam whined. "And just when we were getting somewhere!"

Who were these two? I'd worked around spies my entire career, and I'd never heard such ridiculous statements.

"Maybe she's just stunned." Mark did not sound hopeful.

"Go get the chloroform," Pam barked. "Just in case she comes to."

"But if we knock her out again, it'll take longer to find out what we need to know."

"Go get it!" she screamed.

I heard Mark running away and felt a weight on the couch. Pam was sitting near my feet.

I kicked her, hard, in the kidneys as I got up and removed my blindfold. I was right. It was my neighbor. She was sitting there rubbing her back and staring at me. I took a look around. I was in a warehouse. The only furniture in the room was this sofa and a table maybe forty feet away. A table that held a gun.

Why. On Earth. Did they put it all the way over there?

I ran for it. I needed that gun before Pam realized I was going for it and before Mark returned. Halfway there, something hit the side of my knee, and I went down. Pain was accompanied by little white spots as I scrambled to get back on my feet. Pam was ahead of me by a foot. That gave me an idea.

I ripped off my shoe and hurled it at her head, scoring a bull's-eye. She went down, and I raced past her. The revolver was in my hands, and I turned to see Pam on the floor, rubbing her head, as Mark stood in the doorway staring at us. In his hands were a bottle and a washcloth.

He walked toward us and helped his wife to her feet. They stood there, trying to figure out what to do.

"Who *are* you, really?" Pam asked finally.

"Merry Wrath, Girl Scout Leader," I answered calmly. "But more importantly, I know who you are."

Mark's eyes grew wide, and Pam seethed.

"Isn't that right, Kate Becks?"

CHAPTER TWENTY-TWO

―――――

Rex was there in ten minutes, accompanied by Officer Dooley, who was working his way through a handful of deviled eggs. My eyebrows went up.

"He's on a diet," Rex said quietly. His eyes grew wide at the sight of my face. "You're bleeding! Are those bruises?"

"They'll be gone before the wedding," I said as I waved him off.

Riley showed up a second later with two guys in suits and expressionless faces.

"We'll take it from here," he said to Rex.

My fiancé stepped back and waved the FBI toward the two writhing, screaming spies as I explained what I knew.

"She's Kate Becks?" Rex asked.

I nodded. "I don't know how I didn't see it before. Maybe it was the double-agent thing that blinded me. That might've thrown me off."

"Kate isn't missing because Kate is really Pam, who's a foreign secret agent with her husband…" Rex frowned as he sorted it out.

"That's right." I glared at Riley, who was sending me a silent message to stop talking.

"But," Rex asked, "why did she have two personas in a small town?"

I thought about it. "Mark probably was the one who worked directly with clients. I think the Kate persona was a plant to feed false intel to the FBI."

I stopped the Fontanas as they walked by. "Why did you set fire to the house, knowing you'd left your computer in the secret room?"

Pam glowered at me.

Mark, to my surprise, opened up. "We knew you were in there. We'd been watching the house. When the police left and you didn't, we thought we had a chance to take you out."

"Mark!" Pam screamed. "What are you doing?"

Her husband shrugged. "I'm tired of all this. I don't want to do it anymore." He leaned close to Pam and, in a loud whisper, added, "And if we cooperate, maybe we'll get a light sentence."

These guys really were nuts. That was not how it worked. Sure, in some cases a spy would be deported or exchanged. But these guys were going to an American prison.

"What about the body you saw that night?" Rex asked.

"I think it was a dummy. I saw something like it at Kate Becks' house before the fire." I nodded at Mark and Pam. "It's possible the dummy was a placeholder—someone to make it look like Kate Becks was home. Although, why they chose a naked male mannequin is beyond me."

Mark shook his head. "I knew we should've gotten a female."

"*Shut up!*" Pam screeched.

"We'd just gotten him." Mark ignored her. "The night you were spying on us. We didn't think anyone noticed."

I turned to Pam. "What was with the phone number in the Roomba that Mr. Pickles was attached to?"

This time, Mark glared at his wife. Her shoulders dropped in resignation.

"It's to a burner phone. I hoped the taxidermists would find it and call. Then I'd give instructions for where to send it." She looked at me sheepishly. "I loved that cat."

There was a bathroom in the warehouse, and I used about a dozen paper towels cleaning up my face. The dried blood was a little harder to get off, but I managed. I'd need a shower when I got home.

I returned just as Riley walked over to Rex.

Riley cleared his throat. "Thanks for solving Kate's disappearance."

"You had no idea Pam was Kate?"

He shook his head. He seemed uncomfortable. The always suave, perpetually calm Riley Andrews was a bit shaken.

Rex excused himself to meet the paramedics who'd just pulled up outside.

"Merry," Riley said, "I'm so sorry. I had no idea they'd hurt you."

He reached out and touched my chin, which, according to the mirror a few moments before, was already turning colors.

I pulled back. "This isn't totally your fault. But you are somewhat responsible."

"How's that?"

"If you'd been honest with me about what you were really doing in town, this might not have happened."

An interesting range of emotions played across his face. "I can't give you classified information. I'm with a different agency." He looked pained.

"I get that," I said at last. "Did you know about the Fontanas?"

Riley looked around, but his goons were investigating the empty ropes where I'd been tied up.

"We never saw Pam. If we had, we'd have known she was really Kate."

I had my doubts about that, but decided to leave him his pride.

"It was a pretty good cover. Pretending to be two different people in the same town. Risky though."

Riley agreed. "This will change our investigation. That's for sure."

"I don't want to get you in trouble, but it'll drive me crazy if I don't ask."

A touch of amusement tugged at the corners of Riley's lips.

"Who did they work for? I thought Russia, but my gut tells me that's wrong."

"North Korea," Riley said softly. "Agricultural spies focused on corporate espionage. That's why we think they were here."

I looked at the obviously white couple as they were handcuffed by Riley's guys.

"North Korea? Seriously?" The Fontanas didn't look Korean, but that didn't necessarily matter. Asian countries in particular had, now and then, recruited Westerners for espionage.

Riley nodded. "You of all people should know they have a huge food shortage there." He gave me a wicked little grin. "Thanks for your help, Wrath. See you around."

I watched as he left. Over the door was a clock, and it reminded me that I was in the wrong place.

"Can I go?" I ran up to Rex and asked. "Kelly's going to kill me."

Then Rex did the unthinkable, considering he had a strict policy against any public display of affection while he was working. He pulled me into his arms and kissed my forehead. "I was so worried about you!" He released me. "Officer Dooley will drive you."

The ten-minute drive felt like ten days. Kevin and I never had much to say to each other. He offered me a sparkling water, and I accepted. I thanked him and jumped out the minute we arrived.

"Kelly!" I shouted as I ran up to our booth.

"Where have you been?" my co-leader hissed. "You've been gone for two hours!"

The last attendees were heading toward the exit, and troops were tearing down their tables. "At least I made it in time to help clean up."

I filled her in on my latest exploits, and her fury melted away. She told me to ice the bruises when I got home.

"You suspected Susan, didn't you?" Kelly said with a half smile. When she saw my confusion, she added, "I figured it out when you asked me if I'd told her about Rex."

"I still have no idea how she knew that."

Kelly rolled her eyes, "I figured that out too. You probably listed him as your next of kin on the paperwork you filled out at your first visit."

My jaw dropped. "I filled out paperwork?" I didn't remember that, but I must have. I sighed with relief. Susan was a good guy, and I felt bad for suspecting her.

"How did it go?" I watched as the four Kaitlyns packed up the food. How was it possible that they had éclairs left over?

Kelly grimaced. "It was fine until we declared war on Spain."

Betty! I looked for the girl and found her sitting in the bleachers, arms folded across her chest and scowling.

"It was during the Parade of Nations. Spain was behind us. Betty, Lauren, Inez, and one of the Hannahs turned around and faced the other troop, proclaimed their actions illegal, and declared war."

"We declared war on Spain?" My mouth dropped open. "I wish I'd seen that."

Kelly nodded. "Check YouTube later. Thirty or forty girls had their phones on, recording the whole thing."

"What did Spain do after France declared war?"

Kelly stifled a smile in spite of herself. "One of the girls came forward and declared that Spain's oppression of Catalonia was illegal. Then she joined our girls in facing them down. Their leader and I broke it up, but not before Betty threatened the girls with a guillotine. An actual guillotine made of cardboard. I don't know how she smuggled it in."

I sighed. "At least there won't be a weapons charge."

We packed up the vans and waited with the girls as they were picked up by their parents, one by one. As usual, all the Kaitlyns were picked up at once. Kelly and I said our goodbyes, and I made my way home.

The cats were waiting for me when I flung open the door. I gathered them into my arms for a big hug, even though they didn't know they'd been threatened by Mark Fontana. My cell buzzed, and Philby took that opportunity to escape.

Rex asked me to dinner. He said he had a surprise for me.

A few hours later, with a face full of concealer that Kelly had helped me apply, and my black dress (I'd only worn it once—so it was ok), Rex and I stepped into Syma's Greek Restaurant.

"Mom!" I ran to my mother and gave her a hug.

Rex grinned. "She wanted to surprise you."

"I heard you picked out a dress!" my mother said.

We were led to a huge table, even though we were the only people in there. Rex was about to protest, but the hostess had vanished. The three of us sat down at one end, Rex at the head and Mom and me on either side. That was bizarre.

If Mom noticed the black-and-blue jawline beneath my makeup, she didn't say anything. It was great to see her so soon. There's nothing that can cheer you up like your mother. What a nice surprise from Rex!

The waiter brought out a very expensive bottle of wine. He uncorked it and poured a little into a glass. I watched as Rex swirled it around, sniffed it, and then swallowed. He nodded at the waiter, who then proceeded to pour for Mom and me.

I didn't know he knew how to do that.

The waiter whispered something to my fiancé.

Rex frowned. "They told me the bill is already paid. Again. Just like the last time we were here. Judith, I can't allow you to pay for dinner."

Mom shrugged. "I'm not paying for this."

Rex and I looked at each other. What was going on? This was a setup if I'd ever seen one. And I'd seen plenty over the years.

"Then who is…" Rex started to say before his mouth dropped open.

"Rexley!" A loud, masculine voice boomed from across the room. This was followed by a squeal I think might have punctured my eardrums.

A very tall man with a shock of black mad-scientist hair and a very short, plump woman with dark hair came running across the room, arms open.

Rex barely had time to stand up before the giant man and tiny woman crushed him in their arms.

I turned to Mom, but she just winked back.

"What's going on?" I started, but was suddenly crushed speechless by the strange couple.

"Mom! Dad!" Rex stumbled. "What are you doing here?" He barely got the words out as the giant man shook my fiancé like he was a little rag doll.

Mom? Dad?

Mom! Dad! These were my future in-laws!

"This is our place!" The man laughed loudly. Very loudly. Was he under the impression we were deaf?

"We're paying for your dinner!" the woman screeched and crushed me again. My breathing stopped, which was what happened when all the air was forced out of your lungs. It was like being in a vise grip.

My mother had an amused grin, but I noticed she wasn't included in this assault.

The big man boomed, "You must be Merry!" The couple sat down.

Randi and Ronni appeared and joined us. That's when I noticed they looked just like their mother.

"Hello" was all I could think of to say.

Ronni scowled. Randi smiled and nudged her sister and then looked at me. She waited patiently for something.

Ronni fumed but lifted a badly wrapped package onto the table. She rolled her eyes and said very sarcastically, "This is for you, Merry."

The twins looked at me expectantly, so I opened it.

A giant, stuffed Maine Coon cat, poised to pounce on me, stared through glass eyes. At least, I hoped they were glass.

"Oh!" I forced a smile. "Thank you! I love it!"

Philby was not going to love it. Did cats have nightmares?

"Thanks to Judy here," Rex's father said (my mother didn't even cringe, and she hated being called Judy), "we found out we're getting a new daughter!" He clapped me hard on the back, and my forehead almost hit the table.

I laughed out loud. Rex thought he was surprising me with Mom, but she was surprising us with Rex's family. He'd been outgunned.

"I'm Milli!" Rex's mom trilled. "And this is Bob! We're your new family!"

Everyone started chattering at once as waiters started bringing out food, family style. I let out a long sigh. I finally got to meet Rex's parents, and they seemed, well, sort of normal. I watched as the twins argued and Milli chattered away with Mom. Bob just sat there and grinned. They seemed nice. Weird, but that's what made them wonderful.

All of my life, I'd been an only child. And my career as a spy was, I had to admit, a bit lonely. Here I was, surrounded by a noisy, boisterous family. And it was everything I'd hoped it would be.

Rex squeezed my hand, and all of the strain of the past few weeks melted away. And even with his hot and cold sisters, and the fact that his dad would have to take on a different name when around Philby, I somehow felt like everything might be okay after all.

As everyone but Ronni (who grimaced throughout the whole dinner) chattered away, I couldn't help but grin like an idiot. Now I had everything—a wonderful fiancé, a big family, a troop of funny and smart little girls, my best friend and my goddaughter, and cats who looked like Hitler and Elvis.

Who could ask for more?

ABOUT THE AUTHOR

Leslie Langtry is the *USA Today* bestselling author of the *Greatest Hits Mysteries* series, *Sex, Lies, & Family Vacations*, *The Hanging Tree Tales* as Max Deimos, the *Merry Wrath Mysteries,* the *Aloha Lagoon Mysteries,* and several books she hasn't finished yet, because she's very lazy.

Leslie loves puppies and cake (but she will not share her cake with puppies) and thinks praying mantids make everything better. She lives with her family and assorted animals in the Midwest, where she is currently working on her next book and trying to learn to play the ukulele.

To learn more about Leslie, visit her online at:
http://www.leslielangtry.com

Enjoyed this book? Check out these other reads available in print now from Leslie Langtry:

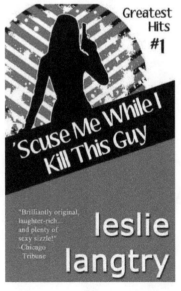

Printed in the USA
CPSIA information can be obtained
at www.ICGtesting.com
LVHW090747260524
781439LV00036B/500

9 781986 348553